Summer Vibes In Naptown

By: Nayh Alontrice

Prologue

Bayleigh

"**Y**esssss Bear, just like thattttt."

"Shut up, don't talk." I started ramming shawty from the back. Couldn't believe I was really giving in to this bitch, but she was here, and I needed to take my mind off what the fuck just happened an hour ago.

"I can'ttttt help ittt. It feels so good," she moaned.

I grabbed a fistful of her hair and slowed my stroke down, making sure she felt every inch of my rod. That shit was short-lived though. I heard the front door opening. I hopped out of her so fast and scanned the room for my basketball shorts. I walked out of my bedroom around the same time she walked in.

"Bayleigh, what you doing here ma?" I looked at her, and her makeup was fucked up due to all the crying I guess she was doing.

"I'm sorry, Bear. I didn't think you was gon find out this soon. I was gon tell you," she tried to explain herself.

"Nah, I don't even wanna hear it. You know how I feel about that. You was supposed to be my wife. I felt like I could marry you, and I can't even trust you," I replied.

"Was?" Her voice broke when she said that. Damn, I loved her so damn much, but I felt betrayed; I can't even lie.

"What you want me to say Bayleigh?"

"Say that you forgive me and that we can continue to be together Bear!" Her voice shook the damn living room.

"You gotta go Bay. Just go." I started walking her towards the door and heard another door opening. *Fuck*, I said to myself.

"For real Bear? This what we doing? Not even an hour after you walk out on me, you already fucking somebody else. And, then, it's this bitch on top of that?! Fuck you, Bear!" She walked out and slammed the door.

"Bayleigh!" I yelled but didn't walk out the door. I was hurting, and hurt people hurt people. Doesn't make it right, but she damn near broke my heart. Not too many women get to do that; matter a fact, no woman had done it. I had a lot of firsts with Bayleigh and, even though this was our first major fight, it was also the first time she betrayed me. I turned around and nearly burnt a whole in this bitch's chest with my eyes, "Did I tell you to come out the room?"

"N-no, but I heard another female's voice out he-,"

This bitch had the audacity. "Tia, your best bet is to get the fuck out. NOW!" My voice roared, and she damn near jumped out of her skin as she dispersed in the room to get her shit I assumed. But, after some time, she never came back out. I walked into the room and she was in there sitting on the bed, crying.

"Bruh, please tell me what you crying for? My girl just caught me making the dumbest mistake of my life with your crazy ass," I took my anger out on her.

"It's something I have to tell you; it's been weighing me down and seeing her just made it worse," she sniffled.

"What?"

"I killed her. It was me."

Fuck! Not only did I just make a mistake by sleeping with this bitch, when Bayleigh finds out what she did, it's gonna be impossible to rekindle any damn thing with me and her.

Bayleigh

"You can do this Bayleigh, you have to pay for mama's chemo. She gave her whole life to make yours a better one. Just shake it off." I stared at myself in the mirror and looked myself over. I had my jet-black hair flowing freely down my back. I was dressed in a red laced bra and thong set. It matched perfectly against my honey-glazed skin. This was my debut night and I just hoped that I wasn't rejected by everyone. I mean, I knew I could pull niggas; that wasn't shit to me. But, there were regulars here who knew that they'd be throwing their money to one damn woman.

"Bay, you up next. Are you okay?" My friend, Syn, walked up on the side of me.

"Yeah, I guess, just a little nervous."

"Just remember who you doing it for. You don't have to make this a career. You hear me?"

"I hear you, let's go. Might as well get it over with." Every step I took towards the hallway got louder and louder inside my head. I had a nice sized ass; it wasn't nearly as big as the bitches in here, seeing that theirs was fake as hell. Once we reached the door that led out to the main floor, I felt a hand slap across my ass. I looked and it was an old ass man.

"Girl, don't trip on that. That's drunk Eddie. He'll be kicked out before the night over. Stay right here though; he'll announce you," Syn stated.

I rolled my eyes and saw a security guard walking over to the old man.

"Don't touch the women; we tell you that every night Eddie," the security guard advised.

"Aight, aight," old man Eddie replied.

"Aye fellas, simmer down. Tonight, Sunset got somebody making their first appearance. One of the baddest females I saw in here in quite some time."

There were a few remarks throughout the club, and I shook my head cause now I was gon have a target on my back. "Ain't really much more I gotta say, her set will speak for itself. Everybody, welcome Honey to the stage," DJ Beats announced.

I almost froze where I stood until I heard *Love Like Honey* by Pretty Ricky starting to play. This was my shit and I was ready now. I strutted up the stairs that led to the stage and seductively walked to the stripper pole. I heard a few ooh's come out the audience and I gave a sexy smirk. I placed my right hand on the pole and did a sexy dip, popping my ass on the way up. I placed both hands on the pole and spun around with my legs spread apart so that I could come down into a split. While in the split, I untied my bra, freeing my size C cups. My nipples were alert and perky, probably due to it being chilly in here.

I crawled over to a dude I peeped whose chair was sitting right in the middle of the crowd. He had a $100 bill in between his fingers. I turned to the side and let him tuck it in my thong. That's when I was able to notice that the stage was covered in hella money and I hadn't heard not one boo yet. I figured I'd really give them a show. I was on the dance team in school, so I knew how to move my body. For the rest of my set, I made sure to leave a lasting impression on all of them niggas. The applause was so loud once the song ended.

I picked all my money up and headed back into the locker room. I heard Syn following closely behind.

"Whewwww bitch, you murdered that shit. Them niggas damn near chanting your name." She smiled hard as hell.

"Girl, I ain't even tryna feed into that shit because I don't want it to go to my head. I'm tryna be a professional dancer, not just this type of dancer."

"I understand love. But, this is going to pave the way for sure."

"Not really, you know I'm doing this for my mama chemo so."

"I know boo. Hurry up and get dressed, so we can head to Waffle House or something."

"Okay," I giggled.

I put my regular clothes back on and grabbed my purse. When Syn left out the dressing room, I counted almost $800. I thought that was amazing for my first night. I put all the money in an envelope and put it in my purse. I locked up my locker and headed out.

The bass from the speakers was thumping, and I swayed to the beat as Duke Deuce's *Crunk Ain't Dead* roared through the speakers. The one guy who tucked the $100 in my thong was still sitting in the same spot but on his phone. He wasn't even focused on the stripper who was clearly trying to be seen all in his face. I guess he felt me staring at him because he looked up and we locked eyes. Damn, I was wishing to see him again; he was so fine. Then, I thought to myself and just walked away. See, after Isaiah, I said I was done with hood niggas and he looked like one. That nigga put me through the ringer and, right now, I could only focus on my mama. I walked up to Syn at the bar; she was talking to one of these lame looking dudes.

"Ohhhh, Honey, hey baby. I was just telling this dude I was waiting for you." She pulled me in passionately and I stared at her weird, but not enough to let dude know she was lying.

"Damn, how can I get down with yall?" he asked.

"Boy no, ewwww, get the fuck on." We walked away cracking up.

"Girl, he almost ruined my appetite," Syn laughed.

***

We pulled up to the Waffle House on Pendleton Pike.

"Bitch, I couldn't tell you was so damn hungry you came all the way out East to this one," I said as I got out of the car.

"Man, the other ones ain't that good. I fuck with this one. Plus, it's late as fuck; it may be some ballers out." Syn gave a wicked smile.

"Yo ass always got an agenda, come on."

I could tell from where I stood that it was packed in there. I didn't even think we were gon get a seat.

"Just follow me. I already know what yo analytical ass thinking," she laughed.

We walked in, and she went to a table that was in the back. We were bumping shoulders with some of the hoodest niggas in Nap. They were staring at us like we were fresh meat.

"Girl, you picked the table in the back."

"Yes, that way every nigga saw us when we walked back here."

We heard the door make a noise signifying that someone walked in. I looked up and saw the dude that was at the strip club.

"Oh no." I grabbed the menu and put it in front of my face.

"Girl, what? Who is it?" Syn started edging her neck out trying to see who it was, looking all obvious and shit.

"Stopppppp Syn, that's the dude that gave me my first $100 bill. He tucked it in my thong. He so damn fine." I felt myself get a little moist just thinking about him touching me.

"Shiiit, he looks like he a demolish yo petite ass. He gon tower over you."

"That's how I like it, but you know me and Isaiah just broke up." I rolled my eyes.

"Fuck Isaiah, he got a bitch pregnant on you. And that was three months ago. It's time you spread that flower to somebody new anyway." Syn jumped up. I tried grabbing her to pull her back down, but she was too quick.

"Oh, my God, I can't stand this hoe." I put my head down into my arms on the table. I didn't even wanna come up. I felt like I was in school all over again. I felt somebody poking my arm. I looked up and it was him.

"I'm sorry to disturb you, but yo friend said you wanted to talk to me." He smiled, showing those pretty ass white teeth. His waves were on swim and his skin was so dark and smooth, like dark chocolate. He wasn't too flashy, other than the pair of diamond earrings that was in his ears. Everything else was pretty coo. One thing I did realize was his muscles barging out of his shit; this nigga looked like he would tear my little ass up.

"I'm sorry about that, she does the most sometimes," I admitted.

"Nah, it's all good. She's assertive, which is a good thing. You seem shy, but you weren't on that stage. You sought me out," he replied. I looked away and started blushing. I just knew I was, I felt it.

"Don't be shy, I ain't mean to put you on blast like that," he laughed.

"It's okay. I really can't believe I did that well on my first night."

"Can I ask a personal question?"

"I mean, I guess. If it's too personal, I'll let you know."

"What made you wanna take this route?" I guess he saw the look on my face because he started clearing it up. "By any means, don't think I'm judging because I'm not. Me and my niggas go there all the time, but I just wanted to know honestly."

"Well, my mama is in stage two lung cancer and she needs chemotherapy. She's still working and refuses to quit, so she could just get Medicaid. So, she has to pay for her medical bills and shit." I put my head down again. I felt his hand lift my head up.

"Why you always do that? You got beautiful eyes, so show 'em off."

"Thank you."

"You blushing again."

Laughing, I said, "I knowww. I hate it so much."

"It's sexy."

"We haven't even exchanged names and you're throwing hella compliments my way," I said.

"I'm Bear; what about you?"

"Bayleigh, and I'm guessing Bear is a nickname?" I asked.

"You'd be right."

"Well, can I know the name of who I'm talking to now? Cause with a name like Bear, I know you had to earn that title."

"Smart woman. Nah, but they gave me that nickname when I played football in high school. Believe it or not, I used to be chubby as hell. Just turned all of this into muscle."

"Okay, I see then. Well, Bear, whenever you feel like I'm worth knowing your real name, let me know." I got up and looked down at my phone. Syn and I had been texting back and forth. She ordered our food to go.

"Wait, can I at least get your number? How I'mma see you again?" he questioned.

"It obviously happened tonight. It'll happen soon." I smiled and walked away. I felt his eyes glued to me every second. This man was gon be a problem for me, I could tell, but that made me even more interested.

Bear

"**C**ome on Bear, you know I'm good for it. Just a dime bag."

I was annoyed that this junkie was standing next to me tryna get fronted for the fourth time. "Didn't I say no? Man, get the fuck away from me. You shouldn't even have the balls to step to me with this bullshit after the last time I credited your ass."

"I'm your uncle, so you still should show some respect man. After this, I'mma go get clean," he chuckled.

"Bye Unc." I just walked away from him. He used to be someone I considered a favorite uncle until he got hooked on the same shit he showed me how to sell. Now, I couldn't even go get my hair cut without him hanging out all in front of the One Stop on Kessler, begging and shit. I hopped in my Tahoe and pulled the fuck off. I had a couple runs to make but, first, I had to pick up a drop from this lil nigga I had running the blocks. His name was Isaiah and he had the potential to be a boss but, right now, he had too much personal shit getting in the mix. I'd have bigger plans for him once he got his shit together fully. I pulled up on 29th and Eugene. He and his homeboys were on the stoop rapping from what it looked like. I walked up and they all got quiet.

"Wassup Bear." Isaiah jumped off the porch and extended his hand to me.

"Wassup? You see I told you I was making rounds today. Where's the bag?" I questioned.

"Moose," Isaiah said. The boy got up and went into the house. He came back a couple seconds later with the duffle bag and handed it to Isaiah.

Glaring at him, I asked, "Do I need to check this right now? I'm not liking the vibe you throwing off right now."

"Come on now Bear, you know I'm good always," he responded.

"Speak up bruh, something clearly bothering you," I replied.

Facing his boys, he said, "I need to speak to him alone." They all disappeared into the house.

"They follow yo ass like you they damn owner or something," I laughed.

"Nah, it ain't even that. They just know I looks out. Them my boys from elementary school. But, on a serious note, when I'mma stop doing this regular ass nickel and diming. I got mouths to feed," he explained.

"I understand that, but do you think I got where I'm at just because I felt it was time for me? Nah, I had to put in hard work. And the fact of the matter is, you're not ready."

"What you mean I'm not ready?"

"You got so much personal shit being exploited all over social media with you and ya baby moms; you hotheaded and always spazzing out. You gotta start using this." I tapped the side of my head.

"Yeah, aight Bear. You just the sanest man ever when I just watched you chop a man's head off the other day." Isaiah tried to test me, but I wasn't letting it happen.

12

I pinched my nose and sighed, "I'mma let that one slide, but you got one more time to try and rush me into making decisions."

Without saying another word, I grabbed the duffle bag and went back to my truck. I only let that slick shit slide because I knew he had a lot of shit going on. I wasn't tryna be hard on him; I just wanted him to earn a top spot on my team. I had three main runners that ran the North, South, and East side of Indianapolis: Ice, Dave, and Pax. I was looking for somebody to cover the West side but couldn't find anyone on my team that was ready just yet, so I'd been covering it myself. I wasn't supposed to be in this game initially but, when my father got sentenced to life when he was with my moms, I couldn't let her do all the work alone. She fought me so much on my decision but, once the money started rolling in, she knew it was the best thing for us to do. She hadn't worked in almost eight years now and I wanted it to stay that way. She gave me life and I would always make sure she had whatever she needed.

That's why I felt bad for shorty last night when she told me about her mom's cancer. I just wanted to give her whatever amount of money she needed, so she didn't have to worry about stripping to make the money. I wasn't tryna judge her; I honestly just wanted her to myself. Those niggas didn't deserve to lay eyes on someone as perfect as her. She had the most beautiful hair that bounced with every step she took. The beauty mark on the right side of her nose was so sexy to me. I paid so much attention to her when she wasn't looking; I just know I gotta have her. One thing for sure, I'd be hitting up Sunset tonight because if she was determined to make that money for her mom, she'd be there.

***

My niggas and I pulled up to Sunset and it was jumping as always on a Saturday night. We made a tradition a few years back that we'd always take a Saturday out of the month to just focus on our brotherhood, and that meant going out and having a good time. Usually, we'd take a couple females back with us to my crib but, of course, I was on a mission tonight, so I'd already set some shit up.

"Damn, they got the fine bitches out tonight. I came in here on Tuesday and they had real life mutts running around this mafucka," Ice said and we all started cracking up.

"You stupid as hell nigga, but you right though," Dave added.

"Yo, look at them two over there." Pax nudged me and pointed towards Bayleigh and her friend she was with last night.

"I already peeped. Shit, I came in here last night and they were in here. She off limits though," I replied.

"What you mean? That ain't never stopped you before," he laughed.

"Nah, I'm saying, I've already spoke to her. She gon be mine, just watch." I rubbed my hands together and looked on as she owned the room. Her smile was so beautiful. I knew right then and there before the night was over, she was leaving with me.

Bayleigh

I saw Bear, well, Syn saw Bear and his crew walking in. That girl didn't miss anything; she saw it all. But, he was looking good as ever in his dark gray Nike jogging suit. I wasn't about to just rush over there. It wasn't my style at all. I was sure we'd connect sooner than later. I had a lot of requests from guys that was at my set last night. My bankroll was getting bigger and bigger. Soon enough, it was about to look like I had a third titty. I was pretty sure about two hours had past and Bear still hadn't made his way to me. It was coo though because like I said before, I didn't need to be focused on no man any damn way.

Interrupting me out of my thoughts, someone grabbed my arm. "Wassup baby, can I get one of those dances?" he asked.

Snatching my arm away, I replied, "Excuse me. You don't have to grab on me for that."

"Come on stuck up bitch, just a quick dance." He got up and started walking towards me. He clearly was drunk but, still, these mafuckas act like they didn't know the damn rules.

"And the answer is hell no, go ask someone else." I turned my back to him and started walking the opposite direction. That's when I heard his voice.

"Aye man, she said no, so just gone on about your business," Bear demanded.

"Who the fuck is you, youngblood? You don't scare me, lil nigga," the man replied.

I turned around and looked on.

"You heard what I said, now move around."

"What, you gon make me, punk ass lil nigga?!" The man was so damn drunk, he didn't even see the shit coming.

POW! I jumped so hard. Bear punched the shit out of the man and then did a signal in the air. The security guard came over and picked the man up off the ground; I was guessing he was about to throw him out. Even though I was damn near turned on by Bear defending me, I didn't need a man to fight my battles all the time. That's exactly what these bitches in here gon think of me. They already thought I was stuck up because I was not rough around the edges. Syn ran over to me.

"Girl, is you okay? I saw this shit happening over from the bar."

"Yes girl, just another drunk ass nigga." I rolled my eyes. Bear turned around and headed in my direction.

"Girl, here he come," Syn whispered.

"Sssshh," I said.

"You aight?" he wondered.

"Yes, I am. I didn't need you to do that Bear."

"What you mean? He was out of line; they know the rules in here."

"I understand that. But, he was harmless. I would've been able to handle it." I looked down at the ground.

"What I tell you about that? Aye, can I speak to her alone please?" Bear turned to Syn.

"Yeah, if I can get introduced to that fine ass dude over there in your crew." Syn pointed.

"Oh, Pax? Hell yeah, gone over; he expecting you anyway."

"Good," Syn chuckled and left us alone.

"So, you were just waiting to play hero? It's been a good two hours since I saw you walk in," I admitted.

"Ohhhh, so that's what this is about? You mad because we ain't play a game of cat and mouse?" Bear started cracking up.

"I don't see what's funny," I responded.

"You are."

"Yeah okay." I turned to walk away.

"Bayleigh," he said in a boisterous tone that sent chills down my body. I hurried back over to him.

"Why would you say my government all out loud like that?" I whispered in a harsh tone.

"Because you keep playing with me. Quit," he said sternly.

"Quit what?"

"Quit stripping."

"I literally just started yesterday." This nigga was tripping if he thought I was about to quit making money for somebody I just met.

"And? Don't you get it?" He put his arm around my waist, and we moved into the dark hallway. His hands felt so soft on my waistline. Whatever this was, it didn't really seem like I had any control of it and that scared me. I didn't wanna jump into another relationship so soon. Shit, Isaiah still be on my line heavy and that was the last thing I needed was drama. But, with Bear, everything felt so right.

"Bear, what are you doing?" I asked.

"Marcus Cartwright," he stated.

"Huh?"

"Remember you said I'd give you my name when I was ready? Well, I'm ready."

"So, you expect me to just walk up outta here with you because you gave me your real name?" I giggled. He didn't say anything, just gave me that intense look in my eyes. "Okay, let me go get my stuff."

It's like I wasn't even thinking before I spoke. But, I already said I would now, so wasn't no turning back. I got all my stuff together and left out the locker room. All the bitches were looking at me in a weird way. I walked out and Bear was up there by his friends, and I saw Syn laughing right along with them. I hoped she found love because she been playing niggas for way too long and I just didn't want her crossing the wrong mafucka.

Walking up, I asked, "What y'all all laughing at?"

"Nothing, baby girl. I was just letting them know I'm cutting out early, that's all."

"Damnnnn, she got you breaking tradition now?" the light skinned dude with his hair in a ponytail said. He kind of reminded me of Ryan off Black Ink Crew Chicago.

"It ain't even like that bro. Just something I gotta handle, that's all." As Bear was shaking up with them, I pulled Syn to the side.

"Do you think I'm dumb for leaving with him?"

"Hell nah. From what I hear, they are all bosses girl. Pax is fine too, ain't he? I'mma definitely get up on that tonight." She started winding her hips.

"Syn, don't even think about trying to play him or doing that shit that you be doing. You need to find somebody to love." I got serious with her.

"Girl, I'm not gon mess up whatever you got going on with Bear, okay? And speaking of love, didn't you just leave Isaiah heartbroken?" She folded her arms across her chest.

"That's not the same thing and you know it Syn; don't even do that." I glared at her and Bear walked up. "We'll finish this later Syn, forreal."

"Yeah, yeah, happy fucking!" she shouted over the music. I tried to turn around to address that shit, but Bear grabbed me by my waist again.

"Yo little feisty ass gotta learn how to calm down," he laughed.

"That wasn't nothing. Syn knows not to try me like that. She just said something that rubbed me the wrong way. But, I'm sure it came from a good place." I followed him.

"This me right here." He walked up to the all-black Tahoe. He opened my door, and I climbed inside. Once he was in the truck, I could tell he wanted to say something.

"What's wrong?"

"Sometimes, people actually mean what they say, so you have to check that shit when it happens."

"I feel you, but Syn is my best friend and her comment was harmless really. Now, can we talk about why I'm in your truck right now?"

"We about to go on a date."

"A date? It's midnight Marcus," I laughed.

"Time doesn't matter to me. We can go on a date at my house." He smiled. I looked at him like he was crazy. "Not like that, just on some chill shit."

"It better be because I'm sitting on a gold mine and you ain't quite ready for that yet," I smirked. He didn't say a word; he just nodded his head and pulled off.

***

We pulled up to what looked like a mini mansion.

"Wow, this place is beautiful." I examined the living room once we got inside.

"Make yourself comfortable." He dispersed into another room.

I just admired everything down from the ceiling to the décor; it was beautiful. He came back in, but in a more relaxed attire.

"Well, I wish I could be in chill mode too, but I didn't know this was the plan." I pulled on my shirt.

"Don't worry about it. I'm just always on the go, so I be happy as hell when I get to wind down. Come on, let's watch a movie." He motioned for me to follow him. We went through the kitchen and, suddenly, I got déjà vu of me cooking him breakfast butt ass naked. I shook my head to get the image out. That was a damn shame; I felt like this nigga had mind control over me. He started going down some stairs and I stopped at the top.

"Nigga, we going downstairs why?" I put my hands on my hips. He sighed and turned around to come back up the stairs. Without warning, he put me over his shoulder. "Put me down!! You could be taking me into a dungeon!" I yelled.

He plopped me down on the sectional and looked at me like I was slow. "It's a home theater crazy." He started laughing so hard.

"Well, shit, I didn't know." I joined in.

"I see you have a hard time trusting people. That's a good thing though; we did just meet yesterday. But, I can't lie, it feels longer than that."

"It really does, it's lowkey scary." I yawned.

Sitting on the other end of the sectional, he said, "Damn, we know who gon fall asleep on the movie first."

"I know right, and I don't want to. I was up all night. My mama had an episode, so I didn't get much sleep," I expressed.

"Oh shit, do you need me to take you home?" It was so cute that he cared.

"No, the nurse is there tonight. She knows if she doesn't hear Syn's loud ass music that I ain't coming home tonight."

"So, you don't have your own car?" he questioned.

"No, we had to sell both of ours due to needing money for her treatment." I couldn't believe I just was so quick to open up to him like this.

He grabbed my hand. "You may hate that this is going as fast as it is, but I don't. It's crazy that I met you right when I did. Lately, I been thinking hard about finding somebody to spoil; I think it's gon be you."

"I don't like being spoiled. I'm my own woman Marcus."

"I understand that fully, I really do, but who takes care of you? I can tell you make sure everybody else is good before yourself. I just wanna show you the good life and take away every worry in the world that you have."

I didn't say anything; I just stared at him while he spoke to me. I couldn't believe this was happening all over again, but I was ready for this. For love, real love this time, not some hood rat ass drama like I endured with Isaiah.

Syn

"**G**et this pussy Paxxxxx, yesssssss, oh my Godddd," I moaned as Pax gripped my waist as I rode his dick. I started grabbing my titties and licking my own nipples, as he held me down and started pounding in me from underneath.

"You like this dick, don't you?" he asked and, in one swift motion, he flipped me over so he could hit me from behind. I wasn't the type to give a nigga the satisfaction of hearing me bow down during sex, but something about his dick was wicked enough to bring me to it.

"Yessss, I love that dickkkkk," I blurted out. He slapped me on the ass and slowed down his stroke, managing to hit every single spot. My body started pulsating and I was ready to cum and go straight to sleep afterwards.

"Shit, shit, shittttttttt." I heard him groan out as he pulled out and came all over my ass.

I collapsed onto my stomach. This was some good ass sex. We had kicked it a little bit but, after a couple of blunts and some Remy, we were down to fuck. He got up and went into his bathroom, then came back out. I felt something warm against my ass. Damn, why did he have to do that? I feel like any nigga that can make sure you're cleaned up after sex really gave a fuck about you. Or maybe he just didn't want the shit to get on his sheets; who knows with these niggas? He laid in the bed beside me and pulled my back into his chest. Cuddling? Was this nigga cuddling with me right now? I had to admit, Pax was sexy as hell. He reminded me of Pooch Hall from that show The Game. And his body was almost identical to his. I could lick ice cream off his 8-pack.

"I get it now," I spoke.

"What?"

"I was wondering why you were wiping me off. I see it was cause of the cum not being on your dick when we cuddled," I snickered.

"Girl, shut yo ass up. I did it cause you ain't just no cum rag," he said in a sleepy tone.

"What does that mean?" I really wanted to know. But, before I could get an answer, I heard snoring.

***

I woke up when the sun started shining through the blinds. "Fuck," I said under my breath. I got out the bed and saw that Pax was still asleep. Even though he looked like a Greek God right now, I had to go. I was going to be late. I did decide to leave him a little note on the stationary I saw on his nightstand and, then, I bounced. I hurried up and pulled up to my mama's house. He was already looking out the window for me. I parked the car, and he ran outside.

"Mommy!" Jr. shouted.

"Hey baby!!" I picked him up and gave him the biggest hug.

"Mommy, I missed you."

"I missed you too, baby! It's been what, a month?" I asked him.

"Thirty long days mommy. Why did you have to be away that long?" Jr. looked so sad. His father was killed when he was only two years old. Now, he's six and getting smarter by the day.

"I just needed to work nonstop, so that we could finally get a big house of our own."

"Yayyy! With a backyard?"

Laughing, I answered, "Yes baby and we can get a pet too, whatever you want."

"I see you still were late, even though we planned this two weeks ago," my mother said in the front doorway,

"Hello to you too, mother," I said as we walked into the house.

"I'm serious Shar. You don't know what I had planned today."

"Mama, it's literally 8:15 a.m. We agreed on 8 a.m.; you act like I'm an hour late. Everybody can't be as punctual as you, mother." I plopped down on her couch.

"Girl, don't plop yo ass on my couch like that! Now, don't forget, I want y'all to come to church with me and Gina."

"Mamaaaa, me and Bayleigh don't do church," I whined.

"Well, she definitely needs to start. I come there and pick Gina up anyway; y'all can come right along. How she not gon go to church with her own mother when Gina is going through what she's going through?" My mama was always so judgmental. She never took the time to understand anyone's point of view but her own.

"I will let her know and we can think about it. Is that fair enough?"

"I guess so. What y'all want to eat tonight? I'm thinking lasagna." Here she goes trying to play fun mama for one day.

"That's fine with me, but I work tonight."

"Noooo, mommy, please don't go," Jr. cried.

"Okay baby, I'm not leaving this time. Just work, nothing more."

"You're always leaving!" he yelled and then ran into his room.

"Mama. Have y'all really been spoiling him like that? He having outbursts and tantrums now?" I questioned.

"Aht, aht, don't even do that Shar. You know he has separation anxiety; he only has one parent. And you were gone thirty damn days! You can take off one damn day of work. I say you have had more than enough time to save up. You can sacrifice a day, seriously." My mother walked out and slammed the door.

I just rolled my eyes. Truth was, I love my son, but it's so hard. I'm only 25 years old and decided to have him at 19. I was in college and couldn't believe I fucked it up. Now, I'm here working at Sunset and I loved it. I would love to cross over into the porn industry, but that would leave a trail behind for my son to know about once he got older. I did have a lot of money saved up, but not enough for a down payment on a house quite yet.

"Jr.!!" I yelled. "GET YOUR BUTT IN HERE NOW!" I heard his door open and he came walking in.

"I'm sorry mommy."

"Yeah, I know. Don't you ever have a tantrum like that again. Do you understand?"

"Yes ma'am."

"Ma'am? Uh, save the ma'ams for your grandma. Mommy will do just fine with me. I'm not going to work later. The whole day is for us. Where do you wanna go?" I asked.

"To the movies!!" he yelled in excitement.

"Perfect, lil man, that's where we going. First, I'mma make us some breakfast and we gon get ready after that."

"Okay mommy."

***

After Junior and I had some breakfast, we took a nap and now it was almost 2 p.m. We got ready and headed over to Studio Movie Grill.

"Mommy, I never been here before." Jr. looked in awe.

"I know baby, we need to start going to new places together. You get to eat your food while watching the movie as well." I smiled.

After we got our tickets, we stopped at the podium to give them to the host. I looked to the left and saw Pax coming out of the bathroom. I hesitated before speaking because I didn't know if we were on that level and I did just leave him with a note.

"Hey Pax," I said, pulling Jr. closer to me.

"Wassup, who's this?" He knelt in front of Jr.

"I'm Jr. and who are you?" my son questioned back.

"Hopefully, somebody you'll see more of. Your mama and I are friends." Pax extended his hand out for my son to shake it. Jr. grabbed his hand and shook it.

"Well, I'm not sure about that just yet. Movie date?" I asked him.

"Something like that. But, what does it matter to you? You left a note on my dresser like the roles were reversed or some sh- my bad."

"Jr., go over and get us some gum balls out the machine." I went into my wallet and passed him two quarters and then directed my attention back to Pax. "First of all, I don't know you like that to be all shaking hands with my damn son. Second of all, I didn't leave that note on your dresser to think you was some type of hoe. I just didn't wanna wake you and, lastly, don't be talking any kind of way in front of my child because that will not be tolerated in the future."

"Yes ma'am but, to clarify, you see me in your future?" he smirked. I started smiling big as hell. "I take that as a yes. So, don't get it twisted lil mama. This little run down you just did don't mean you control shit. Cause we both know who was controlling shit last night now, don't we?"

I couldn't even respond. I just got wet as fuck and damn near became speechless. He kissed my right cheek and then pinched my chin and walked away. He waited by the girl's restroom and a little girl who looked Jr.'s age came out. He walked away with her hand in hand towards the exit. So, that meant they had already watched their movie.

"Mommy," Jr. came to my side taking me out of my thoughts, "I like him."

"Oh yeah? And what do you like about him?"

"I'm not exactly sure, but it just feels that he's a nice person."

Laughing, I said, "Awww, my baby, you growing up. The stuff you say really blows my mind. Let's go."

Bayleigh

I woke up to the sun shining on my face. I guess I had fell asleep while Bear and I was watching the movie. I looked around the basement and he was gone. I grabbed my phone out my purse to make sure I didn't have any notifications. Last night was the first night in many that I was able to fully relax and let it all out. I found out a lot about Bear. He was 32 years old, didn't have any children, and one thing he wasn't afraid to admit was that he was a drug dealer. At first, I was skeptical about him, but I figured he had to be a good person because he wouldn't have done all of this just to string me along.

I figured I might as well prepare myself to leave because he hadn't come back down here yet. While going up the stairs, I started smelling breakfast being cooked. This man knew how to cook too. I walked out of the basement and into the kitchen and was taken aback by who was cooking. It was a woman. She didn't look my age, but she was older. So, he like cougars, I guessed. The way she moved around the kitchen was flawless and she moved as if she lived there. I didn't even say anything, just headed to the front door. When I was headed to the door, Bear caught up with me coming from the hallway.

"Where you going so soon?"

"Oh, well, I don't like leaving my mama alone for too long. And, plus, you clearly have a guest, or I guess I should say she's back home because the way she moves around the kitchen, she has to live here," I explained. He just stared at me and then burst out laughing. I folded my arms and raised one of my eyebrows. "So, you think this is funny?"

"You like assuming shit, don't you? Why can't you just ask questions? Come on." He grabbed my hand and made his way back to the kitchen.

"Hey mama." He kissed her on the cheek and looked at me like I was a fool. "This is Bayleigh. Bayleigh, this is my mother. I know it's kinda soon for all this, but my mama likes popping up and cooking for me from time to time."

"Oh, my God, I am so sorry. It's nice to meet you," I said nervously.

"Nice to meet you too, sweetie. You know, normally, I'd chew somebody out for not speaking when they're in my presence, but you're beautiful, so I'll give you a pass." She winked at me.

"Aight now mama, you ain't about to be hitting on my girl," he laughed.

"Boy, stop playing, you know I don't get down with that. I'm just saying, she's beautiful. You did good son."

I pulled him to the side and cleared my throat, "Umm, your girl?"

"That's right." He was cheesing like a mafucka.

"I'd like to have a decision in that before you claim me. You already got into my mind and I quit my only source of income. Now, you gotta work for this." I winked and walked over to his mother. "It was so nice meeting you; I wish I could stay and enjoy this meal with you both, but I need to get back to my mama."

"I'll drive you. Mama, I'll be back later. I told you to start calling; you don't be knowing what I got going on."

"I hear you, son. Just be careful." I watched her place her hand on the side of his face and kiss his cheek.

***

"This is it right here." I pointed to my house as he turned onto Lancaster Dr. He parked on the curb.

"Well, it's been nice." I was about to get out, but his hand gracefully touched my neck. It wasn't no denying that we had extreme sexual chemistry. I learned that from last night.

Last night

"I've always tried my best to make my mama and daddy proud, and I did. But, my mama got sick and my daddy couldn't deal with it, so he left." I put my head down because I started tearing up. I didn't know how Bear and I got on this subject, but I wished he'd change it. I felt his hand under my chin to lift my head back up. He slid over to me, and I buried my head in his chest and the tears started flowing. I would've been graduated college by now and had an amazing career if I didn't have to take care of my mother. Not saying that it was a burden to me, but facts were facts. My father was a coward and I'd never forgive him for leaving us the way he did.

"Let it out. I can tell this has been held in for a while now babe." He rubbed my back, and I never thought I'd be this close with another man this soon after Isaiah. Truth is,

I was ready to give in to Marcus and give him every part of me, but I didn't wanna be that girl. I mean we hadn't even known each other a week and I was already in his house. "I know what you thinking Bay, because I've been thinking it too. I know we just met, but it feels longer than that. And with my lifestyle, I'm typically not who someone should love, but I can't keep my mind off you."

I lifted from his chest and stared into his eyes. It wasn't long before my lips were on his. I climbed onto his lap and he ran his hands through my hair, which turned me on so much. I sucked on his bottom lip and then started kissing on his neck.

"Damn Bayleigh," he said, almost breathless. I was about to unbuckle his pants, but he grabbed my hands. "You don't know how bad I want you, but not like this. I don't want you when you're vulnerable. I want you when I've had the chance to earn it. Because once I have you, you're fully mines." He kissed my fingers, and I just hugged him.

"I gotta get out this car," I said before opening the door.

"Bayleigh, what's going on?"

"Nothing, you are really amazing but, if I don't get in that house right now, I'm gonna fuck you in your nice ass truck." I bit my lip. His eyes got big as hell.

He got out the truck and met me in front of my house before I could walk in. "Let me take you out, on a real date."

"Where?"

"Leave that to me, just be ready tonight at 8 p.m. I got some stuff I gotta go handle, but just be prepared to have a lot of fun," he said.

"Okay. Bye." I rushed inside the house and put my back to the door. I now knew what people meant by having love at first sight because I damn near loved this man. He was just so smooth, but I also knew that could be a bad thing too. Either way, I was prepared to deal with what came with Marcus Cartwright.

Bear

"There he is," I heard Ice say. I walked into the warehouse I owned off 12th and Illinois.

"What it is?" I shook hands with him and then Pax and Dave. "What's the word?"

"Shit, nothing much. Looks like ya boy Isaiah checked out. The money was all there," Dave mentioned.

"Okay coo," I replied. "Any word on them mafuckas who been selling on Boulevard?"

"Oh, I'mma personally check that shit out myself. Dominic knows to clear with us first before doing some shit like that," Pax added.

"Man, yo ass ain't gon handle that shit. Y'all graduated together. You need to send me over there," Ice suggested.

"Aye man, you not gon keep questioning my decisions," Pax faced Ice.

"Or what? You hesitate too much. Bear knows I'd put two in his dome with the quickness."

"And that's not always the right decision bro. This ain't a standard ass gangster flick. You ain't gotta be the odd one out and wanting to rebel against our plans. This is your chance now; is this where you wanna be? In this crew?

Because you always sound like you wanna be a one man show."

I was getting sick of the bullshit that came from Ice. He always disagreed with any and everything somebody said, he stayed causing friction with us and the other crews out here in Nap and nobody got time for the unnecessary bloodshed.

"You got it, boss. I don't see how suddenly you running shit, when we all agreed to start this shit together."

"Nigga, with the 50k that I raised myself. Y'all my brothers, we grew up together; blood couldn't make us no closer. That's why I decided to build something that we all could eat off." He was pissing me off.

"Aye, I think we all just need to calm down and think this shit through. Why don't Ice just go as backup? That way, if them niggas do try and come at Pax, they won't see Ice coming," Dave recommended.

"Yeah, that's a good idea, I guess. Hopefully, them niggas don't be dumb enough to try some shit cause then we'd both put them in the ground." Pax extended his hand to Ice, and Ice shook it and pulled him in for a brotherly hug.

"Aight niggas, let's get this shit going. I got plans tonight." I was hype as hell.

Laughing, Pax said, "Ohhhh, the Honeybee from the club the other night. I gotta tell you, if she ANYTHING like her friend in the bed, we have lucked up, my nigga."

"Damn, you hit bro?" Dave asked him.

"Hell yeah, and I ain't gon lie y'all. I'm digging the fuck outta her. This may be my new bitch, can't even front," he said as we were packing up our trunks.

"Damn," all three of us said in unison.

"What? Why y'all all in awe and shit?" he questioned.

"Nigga you know why. Yo ass never find love that fast. She must've put a spell on you, real talk," I said.

"Nah, I'm just tired of hitting and quitting these bitches. She different. I can tell she usually be wearing the pants with the fuckboys she used to mess with, but she knows I ain't the one. And she got a son. You know Paris got one child syndrome. With her spoiled ass."

"Don't talk about my niece like that. I told you she can play with her cousins anytime," Ice said.

"She said your kids are like the rugrats. You know her boujee ass mama probably said that shit," Pax laughed.

"Yeah aight, tell her mama don't make me get Tia to whoop her ass talking about our kids and shit." Ice joined in the laughter. We spent the rest of the next hour making sure our next shipments were ready and, then, we all pulled out with our Tahoes full of Indianapolis' finest coke it had ever seen. My life was almost complete. I had the money, the cars; I just needed a family. Bayleigh was gon be that and even more.

***

I looked in the full-length mirror and brushed my waves. I was wearing a dark blue Burberry suit with the black loafers to match. Tonight, I was taking Bayleigh on a date right in my living room. I had Chef Lawrence come in from a conference he was doing in Chicago. Money talked fasho. Let's just say, I paid a lot of money to have him here to cook for us tonight. I found out about him from one of my plugs. I sent a car for her around 7:30 and was waiting for them to arrive any minute now. I turned my phone onto the 90's station and *I Wanna Sex You Up* by Color Me Badd came on.

As if on cue, the doorbell rang. I opened the door and my mouth damn near dropped to the ground. She was wearing a dress that didn't do her body justice. Her nicely pedicured toes stood out in the heels she was wearing. Her beautiful hair was pulled into a ponytail.

"Hi."

"H-hey," I stuttered. "You look amazing."

"Thank you, you do too." She smiled. "Are you gonna let me in?"

"Oh shit, I'm sorry. Come in." I moved out the way and watched her as she walked as if she was on a cloud. Her ass sat up perfectly in that dress and I couldn't wait to nibble on it.

"Really Marcus? The song?" She started cracking up.

"Damnnn, my bad. I didn't even put two and two together." I was about to turn it off, but she stopped me.

"Nahhh, don't even. This my shit though." She sat her purse on the coffee table and started moving her body to the beat, and I just watched in amazement. She turned around and wiggled her finger for me to come to her, and I came. She wrapped her arms around my neck as I wrapped my hands around her waist. "This is nice."

"Yeah, it is," I whispered in her ear. I started nibbling on her ear and I felt her body shutter. Looks like I found a sweet spot. I loved teasing and then eventually giving a woman what her body craved.

"M-maybe we should go eat," she softly spoke.

"Unh unh, relax. Be in this moment that we're in right now. That food can wait." I planted soft kisses down her ear, to her neck, and then her collarbone.

"Ma-Marcus, what are you doing?"

"Sssshhhh." I put my finger over her lips and took her over to the sectional. I took off my suit jacket. "Lean back," I demanded. She did what she was told.

I got on my knees and grabbed one of her legs, softly caressing it and taking my hand up to her thigh, then back down massaging her calf. I looked at her face and her eyes were closed. I watched her reaction as I took my hand all the way up her dress and cupped her ass cheek. She started biting her lip. I pulled the dress up and revealed her sexy bare pussy. I got hard even more knowing that she came over here expecting to get made love to. Her eyes popped up as I entered two fingers inside of her. I knew this was all about her this time. She was so tense and always ready to please everyone else; nobody had pleased her. I let my thumb show love to her clit and her head leaned back as she gasped for air.

"Let it out baby," I ordered. She started moaning uncontrollably, especially when I replaced my thumb with my mouth. I wanted to take my time pleasing her, so I could learn each part of her body. Her hand grabbed my head as I tongue fucked her. She exploded all over my face and I slurped her juices up like I was a dog that needed water. Sensing that she could barely move her legs, I picked her up and carried her into the master bedroom. Once we were there, it's like she got a boost of energy out of nowhere. She ripped open my button up and the buttons flew everywhere. We both started laughing and I lifted her dress over her head, freeing those sexy ass breasts.

"Take your hair down." She took the ponytail out. "You're so beautiful. Them mafuckas at the club would never deserve to see you in this way again."

She knelt in front of me and started unbuckling my belt and then my pants. My dick was protruding through my Calvin Klein boxer briefs. She slid those down and started massaging my dick. That shit felt so good. She took me into her mouth and I almost bust when she slid my dick down her throat. The more attention she gave to the tip, the closer I was to cumming down her throat. I gripped a handful of her hair and started fucking her face back. She pulled me out of her mouth, and I picked her up. I grabbed a Magnum out of my top drawer and had that mafucka ripped and on my dick in two seconds. I slid her down onto my dick and walked over to the bed. I was about to get ready to fuck her, but I wanted to take my time with her. From the feeling she was giving just from walking her to the bed, I knew her shit was a gold mine like she said. I laid her on her back, and we got in the middle of my King-sized bed. I long stroked her and all you could hear was her beautiful ass moans bouncing off the walls. I started sucking on her nipples and her nails were digging into my back.

"Let me rideeee Bearrr, oh, my Godddd," she moaned. I got on my back, and she climbed on top of me and bounced up and down on my dick. I held her by the waist and stared into her eyes.

"Damn, this pussy good," I groaned. She spun around and started riding from the back. I slapped her ass and sat up. I started bouncing her up and down on my dick and planting kisses all over her back. I flipped her over and started hitting her from the back. I grabbed a handful of her hair and our sex sounds were echoing all over the room.

"Yesssssssssssssss!!!!!!!! Yesssss!!!!!!! Bear fuckkkkkkkkkkkk!!!!!!!!!" she screamed. This session started off as lovemaking but turned into what we both really needed and that was to release built-up stress. I gripped her waist and squeezed harder as I released myself into the condom. I collapsed on the side of her and we both just stared at the ceiling.

"That's a nice ass ceiling fan," she whispered. We both started cracking up and she turned to me, "Thank you."

"For?"

"For giving me what I needed."

"And what was that?" I turned to face her.

"You."

I grabbed her hand and kissed the back of it. "Nah, I should be thanking you." We stared at each other for about ten minutes. "I done worked up an appetite, you hungry?"

"Yes. I just need to freshen up a little bit." She stretched out her arms. "On second thought, this bed feels so damn good. Oh, my God."

"I tell you what. After I feed you, I plan on putting you to sleep this time." I winked at her and then grabbed my Versace robe off the hook on the back of my door. I headed to the kitchen but heard some noises outside of my window in the living room. I didn't play that shit. I made sure I kept a good ear out for some sneaky ass shit to happen. I looked at my alarm on the wall and it hadn't gone off, so what the fuck was I hearing?

KNOCK, KNOCK, KNOCK

Somebody was knocking on my front door like the damn police. I bent down and grabbed the 9mm that was behind my sectional and made my way to the front door. KNOCK KNOCK KNOCK. Whoever the fuck this was, was very persistent and was about to get a persistent bullet in they ass. I looked out the peephole and had a bewildered look on my face.

"Is that? What the fuck is this bitch doing here? Fuck." I opened the door and stepped out on the porch to meet this broad before she could walk in. "Tia, what the fuck you doing here?"

"Bear, you gotta talk to Messiah again. I didn't know where to go," she uttered out.

"Nooo, you gotta go Tia. I got in that shit one time and I regretted it the moment I did. Just kick Ice out and you and the kids will be fine."

"No Bear, this time, he kicked me out and he's there with my kids! I don't want him to put his hands on them when I'm not around. You know how far he went the last time!" She started crying hysterically.

"Oh, my God. I told this nigga, man." I pinched the bridge of my nose. "Come on in. We'll have to figure out what to do." I opened the door and there stood Bayleigh dressed in a T-shirt of mine. I had to say she looked good as fuck and I was kicking myself for inviting Tia's ass inside.

"Ummm, who's this?" Bayleigh asked.

"This is Tia. You met Ice, this is his wife."

"Nice to meet you. I wish we could've met on a different occasion," Tia whispered.

"Oh, you're fine. I'll just go put something else on." She looked at me weird and walked away.

"I'm so sorry Bear."

"It's cool, just have a seat. We gon figure this shit out." I went to the bedroom and grabbed my phone off the dresser. I watched Bayleigh as she put on a pair of my basketball shorts. "You sure is finding all my clothes, ain't you? I see you been snooping," I laughed.

"I have not. I just figured you'd have the T-shirts, boxers, and basketball shorts in the drawers there." She joined in laughing.

"I know you wanna ask away."

"It's not my business. I trust you; plus, I'm sure if anybody you were messing with saw me in just a T-shirt, it would've gone differently." She smiled.

"Nah, see this dick I got will make bitches go crazy. That's why I don't give it out all willy nilly."

"Yeah, okay cocky ass. I'll go keep her company while you make your call." She walked out. I put the phone up to my ear, hoping Ice's ass answered. He needed to get it together or leave the girl alone, that simple.

"Aye wassup Bear."

"Wassup is your wife over here crying again. Ice, what the fuck are you doing? You kicked her out man while her kids there?"

"They my damn kids too and she needs to learn to respect me and so do they. She has them undermining my authority every time."

"Bro, I understand all that, but the way she tells it, you try to harm those kids and her."

"She's a damn lie. I never laid a hand on my kids."

"And what about her?"

"I never did it again after the last time bro. Matter a fact, is there something you wanna tell me? Like, why my bitch over there instead of blowing my line down?"

"Don't even try and insinuate some shit. Bayleigh is here and she damn near interrupted what we had going on. So, what you want me to do bro? You want me to send her a ride back home?"

"Yeah bro, I apologize about all this."

"Nah, you good. Aye, what happened with addressing Dominic and them earlier?"

"Oh, shit went well. Them niggas agreed to work underneath us now, so whoever they boss is gon be real upset. We may have a war brewing."

"Aight, that's wassup. We'll handle that shit when we get to it. For right now, we gon keep making money, enjoy life bro. No need to beef with yo woman. If she not who you want anymore, then y'all need to have that conversation, but don't ever get to a point where you gotta lay hands again because you know how I feel about that."

"I hear you, bro."

"Aight one."

I hung up the phone and grabbed my weed case off my nightstand. I pulled out one of the rolled backwoods and lit that mafucka up. These mafuckas was tryna stress a nigga out and I needed to ease my mind and get rid of Tia, so me and Bayleigh could have another round or two. Yeah, I could see us laid up on a yacht making good love. I just hoped she was ready for this type of lifestyle because it was a fast one.

Isaiah

"**F**uck yeah! Right there daddyyyy!" she moaned, as I stuffed my dick in and out her ass.

"You a freak bitch huh? You like this shit?" I asked her while the sweat was running down the side of my face.

"Yessss daddy, I love ittttt."

"I know you love this dick Bayle-," I stopped myself when I realized what I did. Fuck. She stopped moving and I just slid out because I knew what was coming next.

"BAYLEIGH?! Did you just call me that bitch name again? See, Isaiah, I knew yo ass was lying! You not over her!"

"Watch yo mouth. You knew what it was when I called you. I let you know that SHE left me because of yo ass. You lied and said you was having my baby and now look; I lost my girl behind that shit and it ain't no turning back Alexis."

"Cry me a fucking river. You played my ass like a fiddle too. All the shit you promised me and turned our worlds upside down for a soft looking ass bitch," she said through clenched teeth. The vein in my forehead started throbbing. I didn't allow no bitch to disrespect Bayleigh and I never would. I gripped Alexis so hard by her hair.

"Bitch, I told yo ass to stop calling her names. Like I said, it was your fucking fault. So, yeah, I ain't over her yet, but who's to say the more I keep fucking you, that it wouldn't happen?" I kissed the side of her face.

"Fuck you, Isaiah!" She hopped off the bed and ran into the bathroom.

"Yeah yeah!" I yelled after her as my phone started ringing.

"What up tho? Who this?"

"Aye bro, it's Dominic. They on to us."

"What you mean?"

"I guess Bear had Pax and Ice come on Boulevard to try and shut our shit down. But, instead of them just coming all hostile, they asked us if he wanted to die or work with them instead."

"What you niggas say?

"Well, it's pretty fucking clear bro. I'm talking to you, ain't I?"

"Man, put Bones on the damn phone."

"That's the thing bro, Bones wouldn't. They killed his ass."

My heart fell in my chest. That was my baby cousin. He shouldn't even had been in this shit; it was all my fault. I was just taking one L after another one.

"Isaiah? Bro? You still there?"

"And none of y'all tried to save him? Y'all just let my little cousin get gunned down?"

"Bro, wasn't shit we could do. I'm sorry for your loss, but you knew we'd take some hits when you made a plan to go against Bear. I will tell you, bro; I'm on your side still, just working from inside the operation. And I think you'll be pleased to know that one of their own is thinking about joining us."

That was all I needed to hear. I smiled big as fuck. I finally got the chance to bring Bear's ass down. I was so sick of him acting like a good Samaritan and shit but, if anybody knew and got on Bear's bad side, they'd know that he could be a total nightmare. That's why I had to make sure my plan would succeed because if it didn't, I knew I'd have a cold and callous death.

***

Something was very off about today as I pulled up to the warehouse off Illinois. I was only here to pick up my work from Bear. Just because I had a plan in motion, I wasn't dumb enough to stop working underneath him. And as much as I wanted to rip everyone to shreds about my little cousin, I knew I had to play chess and not checkers. I parked my car and was about to walk inside, but I sensed a presence. It was just a feeling that somebody was around me. I looked to the left and that's when I saw her. She was waiting inside of what looked like Bear's truck.

"What the fuck?" I said to myself. I walked over to the truck and opened the passenger side door. "Bayleigh, what the fuck you doing in this truck?"

"I-Isaiah, why are you here?" She tried to close the door, but I stayed blocking it from closing.

"Can I talk to you? You haven't been answering my calls," I pleaded.

"Isaiah, what more do you want from me? You went and got another bitch pregnant; I don't take kindly to being cheated on. You can have all of that and, as you can see, I've moved on." The look in her eyes was unclear; to me, that meant she still loved me.

"Come on B, you can't possibly just throw what we had away like that? The bitch was lying! She's not pregnant. I can take you to her, so you can talk to her yourself."

"It's not that simple Isaiah, it's over." She closed the door in my face.

I lost it. "So, you just gon go and fuck my supplier! You a hoe!" I yelled while trying to open the door.

"Get the fuck back Isaiah!" I heard his voice echoing through the air. I turned around, and this nigga was pointing his Beretta at me. All our crew was just staring and looking on.

"Really? So, you fucking my sloppy seconds?" I was livid.

"I ain't know you used to be with her, bro. If I would've known, I would've discussed it with you first before you had to find out like this," he explained.

"Fuck that, this used to be my bitch."

"Well, it ain't now, now is it? Look like she bossed up." Bear tucked his gun back in.

"I don't know why you put your gun away because she leaving with me and you gon have to kill me for her not to."

"You sure about that? Look, I tried to be respectful and let you know this shit wasn't done maliciously but, since you wanna run off at the mouth, the lady can speak for

47

herself. Let's ask her." He bumped into me as he walked over to the passenger side of his truck. He opened the door and she had tears running down her face.

"Bayleigh, tell this clown that what we had was real and that we working on fixing it," I said.

"Isaiah, you're crazy. We are done; I just told you that when we were alone. I'm with Bear now. I'm sorry you had to find out this way, but you betrayed me and I won't forget about that." She slammed the door, and I just stared at her.

"No hard feelings?" Bear extended his hand to me. I grabbed it and shook it. This just solidified my plan. I watched as they pulled off.

"Damn bro. He just embarrassed the fuck outta you," Dominic walked up and said.

"Shut the fuck up. What you doing here anyway?" I asked.

"That's why we were all here. He was only stopping in to meet us; it was supposed to be quick, but you came. I told you they offered us a spot on their team."

"Yeah. Shit is going in the right direction. And she can be a part of this plan. I'd go after her to get to him. She clearly loves him, and he loves her too. Any man in love has a vulnerability that will cause them to lose everything. And I'd be the one he lost to."

Bayleigh

The truck was silent as Bear drove me home.

"Bayleigh, what's wrong? Speak your mind," he looked over to me and said.

"I don't know Marcus. I thought I knew what I wanted. Wait, that didn't come out right. Put it like this. I KNOW what I want and that's you. Everything just happening so fast and I haven't saw him in three months. I guess all the bullshit mixed with good shit just came and interfered in my mind," I expressed.

"I mean, I get it. This ain't easy for me either. I had to stand my ground out there. All the workers were surrounding us, and I couldn't look like a fool. But, Isaiah is like my protégé. I had no idea y'all used to be together," he admitted.

"Do you regret this? Now that you know I'm his ex?"

"Hell no. Look, y'all clearly wasn't meant to be and he didn't know what he had until it's gone now. I think God put you on this Earth for me and vice versa; we just had to find our way to each other."

"Yeah, but I didn't think it'd hurt this much. I like how you handled everything back there though. It made me feel safe. Isaiah is not the Isaiah I used to know. It's like he went crazy for a minute. He kept trying to pry the door open when I closed it. I was actually afraid of him in that moment."

He pulled up to my house and got out the car. He came and opened my door but, before I could step out, he blocked me. "You'll never have to feel that way again. You being with me is gonna influence you. I will get you protection and you will also be able to protect yourself. I just got a question though." He cupped my face with his left hand and rubbed my cheek.

"What's that?" I said breathless. It's like his touch just did something to me.

"Is this, being with me, Marcus Cartwright, what you want?"

"Yes," I responded within a second.

"Okay then, are you ready for me to meet the most important person in your life right now?" He smiled.

I smiled too; I was happy he was willing to meet my mama.

***

"Okay, wait right here. I'm gonna make sure everything is okay," I told Bear.

"Aight, I got you."

I headed up the stairs towards my mama's bedroom.

"Mama, everything okay?" I said as I walked in her bedroom. She was checking her blood sugar.

"Oh, hey baby, I didn't hear you come in. Everything is fine. Nurse Abby left around 8 a.m. this morning" she responded without looking up.

"Oh, well, I have the money for your second round of treatments. So, that's one less thing you have to be worried about." I sat by her.

"And where did you get that type of money Bayleigh Marie?" she questioned and, once again, she hadn't looked my way.

"Ma, what does that matter? I told you it wasn't any other option available."

"There is an option, trust God." She finally looked me in the face.

"I understand that ma, but we don't have all the time in the world and, as selfish as it sounds, I'm not ready for you to just be all, 'if it's my time to go, it's my time to go', spill." I fold my arms and started pouting.

"Oh Bayleigh, you know I wouldn't accept any money that wasn't made legally."

"Mama, I never said it wasn't legally made."

"Yeah, little girl, you never could lie," she chuckled.

"Ma, there's somebody downstairs I want you to meet."

"Finally, I get to meet the man who had you out of the house all week long. How long have you known him?"

"I can fill you in on the details a little later." I was just ashamed to let her know I done fell in love in a short amount of time.

"Is he the one paying for the treatment?"

"No, I earned that money on my own." I felt bad lying to my mama. Truth be told, I only earned enough money for about two rounds of chemo. Bear was paying for the rest of her treatments for the year.

"I don't know Bayleigh. I'm not really feeling up to it today. Shar's mama will be here bright and early to pick me up for church in the morning. Now, unless you both will be attending with me, then we can worry about meeting later down the line when you're sure that you want to be with him. You know you did just get out of a relationship not too long ago."

"I know that mama and, quite frankly, I'm tired of people saying that. I already feel myself that this sh- I mean stuff is happening too fast. But, I really do like him mama. It would mean the world to me if you met him," I begged.

"Well, when you put it that way, have him come by tomorrow after I get back from church. That way I'll be in my Sunday Best and not looking like death."

"Don't say that. Okay, I'll let him know. Thank you, mama." I kissed her on the cheek and left out the room. I hoped Bear wasn't gon be too down about it. I came back downstairs and he was on the couch sleep. My baby must've been tired from all the work he put on me last night. I went into my purse and got my phone out. It had been a couple of days since I talked to Syn and that wasn't normal at all. I dialed her number.

"Hey stranger," she blurted through the phone.

"Girl bye, I can say the same for you. How you doing?"

"Everything is everything. I should be asking you that. Did Mr. get to knock them cobwebs off the punany?" she laughed.

"More like murdered the punany. Girl, I'm in love with this man."

"OOOHHHHH, girl, you are lying! You gave him some already!"

"I know you ain't tryna judge?"

"Hell nah, you go girl! His friend wasn't too bad either, but he being weird now."

"What you mean?"

"Girl, like he wants me forreal. I thought it was just sex, but he looking for more. And, then, I took Jr. to the movies earlier and he was there with his daughter. Well, she was in the bathroom, but he talked to Jr. and everything."

"How did Jr. feel about that?"

"He likes him. I don't know why, but he does. He said he feels that he's a good man for me."

"He is getting older. Oh, my God, time be flying. I saw y'all picture on your snap."

"Yes, he's definitely a handful. My mama and I had words. She keep saying me and you need to go to church with them."

"Same here. My mama just gave me a lecture about God."

I saw Bear's arms in the air while he was stretching.

"I say you give Pax a chance. You need to think about settling down. Shit, we both do. We could do double dates and all that."

"Here you go. We gon see. He wants to meet up tomorrow, so I'll check it out."

"Alright babes, just hit me later on this week. Maybe we can do lunch or something since I'm not working at the club no more."

"Wait, what?"

"I gotta go Syn, love you."

I hung up the phone as I saw Bear walking into the kitchen. He walked behind me and wrapped his arms around my waist.

"I see somebody was tired," I said.

"Yes, I was. I had put in a lot of work last night," he whispered in my ear.

"So, what would've happened if my mama woulda came downstairs with me?" I laughed.

"I had kinda heard y'all whole conversation. Not saying you loud, but you loud." He started cracking up. I playfully hit him on his arm. "Nah, in all seriousness though, I understand where she's coming from. I almost wish my mother was more like that. Instead, she pushed me out into the streets more, especially when my father got locked up."

"Damn, I'm sorry bae."

"It's all good, trust. I can't say I haven't appreciated this lifestyle. But, it definitely comes with its cons."

"Have you thought about if you want this to be what you're doing for the rest of your life? And don't think I'm judging or anything. I just want to know."

"Oh yeah, I have my hand in a few business ventures that'll start me off fresh. That way, the more that income comes in, I can finally leave the drug business alone." He kissed the back of my hand. "Speaking of, I'll have to leave you now."

I tried my best not to look sad or disappointed. "Okay, I understand. I guess I got too comfortable."

"Nah babe, don't even say it like that. You know I rather be with you. But, I can't have you with me doing this shit. I gotta make sure you safe at all times." He kissed the tip of my nose.

"I understand. I gotta go to church tomorrow anyway with my mama, so I'll hit you up after that?"

"Bet. See you tomorrow." He kissed me softly on my lips and I couldn't believe that I was so sad that he was leaving. It was probably best anyway because I felt like I was getting sprung and I ain't like that at all. Then, on top of that, it was about to be summer. Syn and I had a whole plan to be straight hoes this summer, but it looked like we would both be locked down still. I guess it's not a bad thing seeing that we're dating bosses. Only thing I hoped was we didn't get dragged into their business because we're associated with them. But, I will say that Marcus is somebody I'd fight for. And if anybody tried to get in the way of taking him from me or vice versa, it was gonna be a war brewing.

Bear

I couldn't help but start to feel like I was becoming a sprung ass nigga. But, it was all good because I knew I had finally found a real ass woman that would appreciate me for who I was. She was all I thought about and it was lowkey tough without being around her. But, I knew I was going to have to find a balance between my work and personal life. The only reason she was even with me when that Isaiah charade went down was because I left my planner in the office and I needed it. I wasn't the type of nigga who put everything in my phone; that was how you got caught up. I made it a goal to keep my work away from Bayleigh. That was the last thing I needed was for her to get into any crossfire from these hating ass niggas in Nap.

I had an eerie feeling about Isaiah, and I wanted to start watching him closely. I would hate to have to put someone who I practically helped get to where they were now, in the ground. He may have shaken my hand, but I was not someone who was naïve. I knew he still had strong feelings for Bayleigh and, from the look in his eye, he'd do whatever he could to get her back and that could even mean stabbing me in the back. I called Pax and Dave and told them to meet with me at the Flanner House Park. I pulled up and they were both standing outside waiting for me in front of their trucks. I parked and hopped out the truck.

"Wassup, where Ice at?" Dave questioned.

"Look, for now, this operation has to stay between us three. As vocal as Ice has been, always disagreeing with everything that any one of us says, it's only a matter of time before he becomes an enemy of ours," I explained.

"Nah, I don't think he'd be that dumb. I mean, come on now, you helped Ice get everything he has; you helped all of us," Pax commented.

"That's just it though; he's sick of being in the shadows. He doesn't wanna accept that I'm the one who started this shit. I mean, I never made y'all bow down or no type of shit like that and I never will. Every time before now we've discussed shit as one and made the right decision. You can just tell by his actions, the move he plans on making in the future. And now that Isaiah has a reason to go against me, I wouldn't be surprised if they were in cahoots."

"Well, I understand why you're questioning Ice's loyalty, but I don't think we have enough evidence as of now. If Ice has a plan to become an enemy of ours, we'll see it. He'll reveal his hand sooner than later. As far as Isaiah goes, he's a small fry itching to be something bigger. There's no telling what he got stirring up," Dave added.

"Yeah, those types of niggas can't wait to make a big move and cause a scene. Shit, I wouldn't be surprised if he'd try and recruit one of us or some shit." Dave and I both stared his ass down. "Nah, don't even look like that. I'd never go against the grain; I'm just keeping it 100. That nigga gon be so arrogant that he'd feel like he could ask one of us to join his team. Just watch."

I took everything that Pax and Dave said and stored it in my mind. For now, shit would operate as normal, but we'd have our third eyes open. There wasn't shit that was gon get past me and I'd hate for a mafucka to make me show them why the streets kept my name, Bear.

***

I woke up to someone knocking at my door.

"What the fuck?" I said, wiping my eyes. They started knocking again. I hopped out the bed and grabbed my robe off the back of my door. Once I reached the door, I looked out the peephole and shook my head as I opened the door.

"Tia, what now?" I asked.

"I need your help Bear. Ice is out of control and I don't know what else to do." She barged into my house, and I thought about going off on her ass but thought against it. I just closed the door instead.

"So, what you think I'mma be able to do? He's a grown ass man and you're a grown ass woman. Just do what you gotta do to keep you and your kids safe. You can't keep coming here."

"I'm, I'm sorry Bear. I didn't mean to intrude. I just know you're one of his best friends and he listens to you," she vented.

"According to him, he doesn't lay hands on you, Tia, so what is this really about? I've had a long day and I'm exhausted," I admitted.

Sighing loudly, she said, "Well, truthfully, I believe I can help you in return for you helping me."

"And by help, what do you mean?" I was intrigued.

"Truth is, after the first incident, Ice never really hurt me again. The only reason he put me out was because he found out I had feelings for someone else. He doesn't know who, but he knows from my journal," she explained.

"You grown as hell with a journal?" I chuckled.

"It's therapeutic to write down my thoughts. I can't really talk to Ice like that. Ever since he got shot four years ago, we just drifted apart. I don't know why the kids kept coming because I stopped loving him a long time ago."

"I understand that you having an epiphany or something Tia, but this really doesn't sound like some shit I should be hearing."

"That's just it. You're the exact person who should be hearing this. Bear, I fell in love with you ever since you helped me and the kids when Ice was down. You made sure that our bills were up to date and that my kids wanted for nothing."

"Tia, that was all out of love for Ice. He's like my brother so, yes, him getting shot caused me to look out." I folded my arms and looked at her in a confused manner.

"I know, but I couldn't help but fall in love. You were so nurturing and caring; you truly didn't live up to your name. In the streets, people are real life scared of you, but that's not what I see." She walked over to me and put her hand against my face. Then, she put her hands inside my robe and moved them down my chest. I stopped her once she tried to touch my dick because Bayleigh's face popped in my head.

"Noooo, Tia, this ain't a good idea. You need to step." I started walking to the door.

"Please Bear, just let me get a taste of what drove your exes insane. I only got a teaser back then. I need that type of dick in my life. Ice can't give me that anymore," she pleaded.

"Well, ask someone else. I'm out of commission." I opened the door and motioned for her to get out.

"So, who you with? The chick that was here the other day? Yeah, she a little cutie, but she don't look like she can handle all of you. She's not ready for the type of lifestyle you live."

"You don't know shit. And I ain't about to entertain you any longer, now bounce."

"Fine. But, the information I have on Ice is gonna cost. And since you won't pay me in dick, money will do." She winked at me and started walking away. This bitch was truly crazy as fuck, but her saying that just let me know that Ice was planning some bullshit. It was all good though because I'd use her ass. It wasn't nothing to come up off a couple bands to make her talk.

Ice

I was walking back and forth waiting for this bitch to finally show up.

"Nigga, can you calm yo ass down? You making me all jittery and shit," Isaiah said.

If looks could kill, he'd be a dead mafucka right about now. I stopped at my desk and separated two lines of coke. I did them both back to back.

"AAAAHHHHH, that's more like it," I laughed.

"You need to slow down on that shit. Can't believe you be getting high on yo own supply."

"Nigga, did I ask you to come in here and be Dr. Phil and shit? I don't care about you judging me, nigga," I said to Isaiah through clenched teeth.

"I'm just saying. I can't afford to fuck up what I have going on all for you to fuck it up. I don't need you acting like a mad man. We have to succeed with this plan or we're dead."

"You sound like a coward. You should never be afraid of any man."

"It's not even that bro. I'm just tryna make sure this shit goes right."

He was lucky I heard the door open. Tia came rushing in.

"So," I said to her.

"It failed. He wouldn't budge," she admitted.

"Shit, should've never let you do it any damn way. You're washed up."

"Fuck you, Ice! I should've never agreed to help yo ass any damn way." She stormed out of my office.

"What exactly was getting her over there going to do? Bear is more advanced; he's in the big leagues. There's no way a piece of pussy is gon get him to fuck up or have diarrhea at the mouth," Isaiah expressed.

"You may be right, BUT, there is a piece of pussy that'll get him knocked off his square." I watched Isaiah as the vein on the side of his head started to throb.

"Don't even say her name."

"Shit, I don't know her real name. I know her stage name is Honey. But, it seems like she's the person that can get him out of that element. I say we go after her."

"She'd never go against him."

"Who said we wanted her to comply to be a part of our team? I'm saying we'd threaten or kidnap her to make him give up his seat on the throne. That way, people would have no choice but to be supplied through us. He'd exist no more."

"Good luck with that. I won't harm Bayleigh though. That day she chose him over me, I said I didn't care what happened to her, but I do. So, if that's gon be your plan, then you can keep me out of it." He stood up and prepared to walk out.

"Fine, your decision, I can't argue with that." He stopped dead in his tracks and shook his head. Without warning, I pulled out my 9mm and shot him in both his legs. He fell to the ground and started sliding to the front door, leaving a blood trail in my damn house.

"There you go, you almost there," I egged him on. Then, I shot him in his spine. My goal was to paralyze him and that's exactly what I did. Well, of course the doctors would have to say it, but I didn't want this mafucka to die. Not now. See, that's exactly what Bear would be losing, a skilled shooter, which was me. I trained in this shit; I learned all about guns and the human body. I know the right places to hit to assure that the person wouldn't die, only suffer. I put Isaiah in the back seat of my truck and sped to the hospital. Once we reached Clarian Hospital, I opened the back seat and sat him on the ground in front of the main doors. And as quickly as I did that, I pulled off. His cries were loud and annoying as hell. I was just happy to have him out of my damn truck. Of course, if he'd go to the police or even if they tried picking his case up, they'd have a hard time finding out who did this to him. Before we left my home, I covered the license plate and had a scarf wrapped around my face with a hat on. So, I wished them the best of luck. Tia came downstairs all frantic, but I threatened her too, so now she's at the house cleaning up the blood. I was ready to go down a path to take what I felt like should've been mines. And there was more blood to spill than Isaiah's, that's for sure.

***

I woke up sleep inside my truck in the driveway of my own damn house. Damn, I must've really been high as fuck because I usually wouldn't be caught lacking like this. The sun burned my eyes as I walked up to my front door. I never questioned myself for any of the decisions I'd made, but I felt like I probably made a drastic decision by turning against Isaiah. That was my only ally right now and I decided to let my temper get the best of me. I knew it wasn't any turning back from that decision, but only I would know that I made the wrong decision with that. Nobody else would ever know. I tried unlocking the front door and my key wouldn't turn.

"What the fuck?" I said out loud. I tried it again and it did the same thing. I know this bitch didn't get the locks changed for the house I purchased. I started banging on the door like I was the damn police. I heard the locks being undone. Then, she appeared through the crack of the door with the chain still on it.

"What Messiah?" She glared at me.

"Open the goddamn door! You don't change locks on the house I pay for! Have you lost your damn mind?" I yelled.

"Nah, but you have! You think I'd let you come back in here with my children after the shit you pulled last night!" she shouted back.

"Tia, come on now, this is federal as fuck. Let me in my own house and we can discuss this shit quietly," I begged.

She stared at me for about thirty seconds and then finally let me in. I closed the door behind me, and we just stared at one another. In one swift motion, I had my hand around her neck. I lifted her off the ground and saw the veins coming to her forehead.

"If you ever try some shit like that with me again, you won't make it to see any of our kids graduate. Do you understand me?" She barely managed to nod her head up and down. I threw her to the ground. "Matter a fact, you're useless. I think it's best you and the kids move into your own place. I'll pay child support; shit, I'll even stay out of your lives. It'll reduce the burden that's on me anyway."

I walked away from her ass, leaving her there sobbing. I walked past the kitchen and the kids were staring at me at the table eating their breakfast. I had three kids with Tia and, at one point, I did love her and them. This life was what I wanted at first but, the more I became a part of this lifestyle, the more selfish I became. I think them being away from me would be best for their sake. And with the plans I had coming, I couldn't allow them to be in the way or get me caught up. I walked over to them and kissed them on top of their heads one by one.

"Daddy, are you and mommy getting a divorce?" my youngest daughter, Mia, asked.

I laid my hand on her shoulder. "Oh, baby girl, we are breaking up. But, I promise you all will be taken care of. Sometimes people grow apart and me and your mother have been together for a long time." My daughter put her head down and started sniffing; I knew she was crying.

"No Mia, don't shed a tear for him. We will be okay without him; he wants to sit there and treat mom as if she's nothing. Keeps laying hands on her; you see my little sister is too young to understand that you're a monster. I saw what you did to that man last night. You don't even care about the fact that you had four witnesses in here last night. I can't wait to graduate high school, so I can leave this shameful ass life!" my oldest son, Messiah Jr., yelled. My eyes were big as day. He never spoke to me that way before, let alone in that type of tone. I was really kicking myself in the ass now because the coke must be the only reason I even did that shit while my kids were here.

"You wanna say that shit again son? Don't make me do something YOU will regret." I walked up to him. My son was damn near the same height as me now at 15 years old.

"What you gon do? Kill me next? Your own son?" He stared me in my eyes.

"Nooo!" Tia ran in the kitchen and stood in between us both. "Mia, William, go and get your stuff together, now!" She turned to Messiah Jr. "Listen to me, baby, this is my fault for staying in this for so long. I promise we will have a better life without him. Now, go and get your things."

Messiah Jr. walked off and she turned back to me.

"You will rot in hell for the way you treated me and the things you said to our son. Just know that what goes around comes around." She stormed off. I started laughing hysterically. Fuck it, I didn't need anybody but myself. Losing them was the sacrifice I had to make to be the boss. Naptown would be seeing a new kingpin and his name ain't Bear.

Syn

It was Sunday morning and, of course, my mama demanded I'd go to church with her. I mean how could I not give her what she wanted and she's helped raise my son? I looked down the aisle and there sat my mama, Ms. Gina, Bayleigh, my son, and then me. I felt like I was wrong for sitting in the house of the Lord knowing that I sin at least 22 hours out the day. But, I knew he would forgive me once this part of my life was done and over with. I grabbed Jr.'s hand and kissed the back of it as the choir beautifully sung. Tears started falling down my eyes. This was why I hated coming to church; it made me so vulnerable. I wasn't born into a life where everything was automatically okay for me. I used to wake up to my own damn father molesting me. It never got to the point to where he could rape me because I opened my mouth. I told my mother what was going on and she chose me. He got locked up for it and didn't really have to do too much time, but he's a registered sex offender. He called literally every Sunday and left my mother a voicemail on her landline. I don't know why he thinks we'd ever be able to overcome that.

"Today, saints, I want to talk to you all about forgiveness. Because we all know that holding in pain and suffering from what others have done to you can hinder your life." I couldn't believe this was his topic today. I literally just thought about all of this. "My goal for you all today and the title of my sermon today is "Let That Hurt Go." You got to let it go because if you don't, you'll never successfully move forward in life."

The room roared with applause. For the next hour, we just listened to him explaining how forgiveness could break all the shackles that have us bound. I wanted to go up to the altar, but I was afraid. Bayleigh came over to me and held my hand.

"I'm scared too, maybe next time." She did a half smile. I squeezed her hand and just laid my head on her shoulder.

    ***

We were at my mama's house enjoying Sunday dinner.

"So, Shar, do you know anything about this new man my daughter been seeing?" Ms. Gina asked me.

"Oh, yes. He's a nice guy, Ms. Gina," I replied with a fake smile.

"Girl, you can't fool me. What's the deal with him?" she questioned.

"Ma! Please, there's nothing wrong with him; he's really a nice guy," Bayleigh pleaded.

"Yeah, okay."

"No, forreal Ms. Gina; he's a nice guy for Bayleigh. I even date his friend. We met them together at th-," Bayleigh elbowed me in my side, "we met them at Waffle House." I smiled.

"Oh okay, well, like I told her, maybe if he makes an appearance today, I'll be willing to meet him." She looked at Bayleigh and smiled.

"Thank you, mama. You know if you don't meet the person I love, I can't be with them. You're the most important person in my life." She walked over to her mama and hugged her.

"I love you too, baby girl."

I got up and went looking for my own mama. We had so many disagreements over the years, I wished our relationship was like Ms. Gina and Bayleigh's sometimes. I heard her snickering with someone over the phone in the kitchen, but it looked like she was hiding it.

"No, I haven't told her yet. But, I will on my own time. You know how I feel about being rushed," she said to the person on the phone.

I snuck up behind her and was about to interrupt until I heard the name she stated.

"Gene, I will, just gotta give me some time." My eyes watered and literally started stinging. I couldn't believe that she would even speak to him and, from the tone of the conversation, they were getting along. After all he did to me. My heart shattered. And to think the pastor wanted to preach about forgiveness, but how could I ever forgive someone who speaks to the man that scarred me for life? I let out a gasp and covered my mouth. She turned around with the most shocking look on her face.

"Shar, Shar baby, I can explain. Please let me explain," she begged.

"NO!!!!!!!!!! All this fucking time you've been speaking to him! And to think you let me believe you believed me!!!!!!!!!!! I thought you chose me!!!!!!!!" By this time, Bayleigh was in the doorway of the kitchen.

"Watch your tone Shar! I am still your mother!"

"Not anymore! Jr., let's go!" He came running out of his room.

"Mommy, why are you crying?"

"Don't worry about that baby, just let's go. We'll get your things later," I told him and grabbed his hand.

"Those are things I purchased for him when he was living with me. You're not taking any of it," my mother responded.

"We don't need it. I don't even want shit you got or bought. Burn in hell." I put Jr. in the backseat of the car and got in the driver seat. Bayleigh hopped in the passenger and I sped off.

    ***

I sobbed uncontrollably as Bayleigh rubbed my hair. I had my head laid on her lap. She had set Jr. up in her bedroom watching TV. We were in the living room.

"Syn, how do you know if she was talking about being back with him or not?" I asked.

"Bayleigh, that's not the point. The fact that she is even speaking to him is messed up seriously. I had to go without having a father. Even after they divorced, she still didn't re-marry. It's like were you still in love with him after all these years, even after what he did to me?" she expressed.

"Yeah, I understand, it's very fucked up. You just need to take all the time you need to see if you really want your mom out your life. You only get one mom, Syn."

"I know." I dried my eyes and sat up.

"Oh shit," Bayleigh said.

"What?" I asked.

"I forgot I told Bear to come over and bring Pax. I thought he was gon meet my mama today."

"Nooo, I can't let Pax see me like this. And Ms. Gina will be home any minute. I'm sure my mama is about to drop her off. Why don't we just go over there?"

"That may be a good idea lowkey. But, what about Jr.?" she asked.

"I don't know. I don't fuck with my mama right now; he'll just have to come along. Pax already met him."

"Okay, let me call him then."

"I'll get Jr."

***

Not too much was said on the way to Bear's house. I was just happy on the inside about seeing Pax. I didn't wanna let that shit show because then, I'd turn into a different type of bitch and I wasn't ready for all that. I looked in the backseat and Jr. was sleeping peacefully. I didn't want to keep him from his Granny, but he'd forgive me one day. It'd take a miracle to help me get over the betrayal from my mama. But, I felt like I should stop thinking about this shit right now as we pulled up to Bear's house.

"You sure you up for socializing? You know my mama wouldn't have tripped if you and Jr. stayed at our house," Bayleigh said.

"I'm fine B. Let's just go inside. I need to take my mind off this shit anyway."

Once we were out the car, I held Jr. in my arms while we waited for them to answer the door.

Opening the door, "Hey ladies," Bear smiled at Bayleigh. "And who's this?"

"This is my son. My bad, I didn't have anyone to watch him," I explained.

"No need for explanations here; we gon all be family anyway." Bear moved to the side to let us in. I watched as Bayleigh blushed her ass off.

"Is there anywhere I can lay him?" I questioned.

"Yep. Pax, why don't you go ahead and show her the guest room?" I eyeballed Bear as he just volunteered Pax's services and that nigga didn't even acknowledge me.

I followed him to the back room and it damn near looked like two rooms in one; it was huge. I knew my baby was gon be sleep for hours on this damn bed. I laid him down and then kissed his cheek. I looked up and Pax was leaning against the wall, smiling.

"What you all cheesy about?"

"It's nice to see you in this type of setting," he replied.

"What do you mean?"

"Mothering. Being a nurturer and not somebody who always have to be tough."

"I mean, that's when I'm out in the streets or at the club. You can't show vulnerability there."

"It's a dog eat dog world, I get it. But, what about when you be with me?"

"That was only one-time Pax." I crossed my arms.

"I understand that. I want it to be more though," he stated.

"Why though? I'm nobody special. Just little ol me," I giggled.

"That I want and, no matter what you say, I'm gon keep trying until you realize it." This nigga started inching his way towards me.

"I'm saying though. I have a lot of baggage that comes with me. I just found out some bullshit today. I'm not sure this is something you want to pursue," I confessed.

"Why don't you let me make that decision for myself?" By this time, he was close enough to devour me. He planted his lips on mine and I melted in his arms. Tears started staining my cheeks and I didn't even realize it. I just knew that this was the safest place I had been in a while. I decided to do what I did best, and that's please a man. I didn't feel comfortable having sex while my son was in the room, so we moved to the next guest room. I prepared to take my clothes off, but he stopped me.

"What's wrong?" I asked.

"As much as I want you, in the worst way, I'd be an ass for doing that. You clearly hurt about something, so just talk to me."

"You wouldn't even look at me the same."

"You right. I'd look at you with even more respect for opening up to me. I got you, Syn, from here on out. Shit, what you want me to do? You want me to scream that shit out? Huh?" He hopped up off the bed and opened the guest room door. "AYE, Y'ALL CALL ANYBODY YOU WANT, TELL THE WORLD, SYN IS MINE NOW AND I'MMA MAKE HER THE HAPPIEST WOMAN IN THE WORLD!"

I was cracking up; he played too much.

"We know!" Bayleigh and Bear yelled back. Pax closed the door back and I had happy tears running down my face. We just sat there and talked for the remainder of the night. I told him everything that hurt me and he knew my fears.

Bayleigh

"I just can't get over how beautiful this house is, seriously." I was sitting on his sectional with my legs tucked under my butt.

"Thanks, my mom helped me decorate and everything when I first got it. I want you to be comfortable here though, so make yourself at home." He sat by me and placed his arm on the back of the couch.

"Can you tell your mom I'm sorry we had to leave like that when she was here? I would've loved to enjoy that breakfast she cooked."

"She ain't worried about that; she knows she comes over unannounced and that needs to stop. Especially since I got a girlfriend now."

"Oh, you do?" I smiled.

"I do." He leaned in and gave me a peck on the lips.

"I'mma stop playing then," I started laughing. "I'm happy to be your girlfriend."

"Good, because I knew you was gon be mine when I saw you, no lie." He started showing those pearly white teeth cheesing like a mafucka.

"So, you just knew I was gon fall into your charm?"

Chuckling, he responded, "Charm? You make it sound so proper, but you know it though."

"Yeah aight. You were the one hooked by me."

"Mmhmm, you know I was. I can't even front."

We started cracking up.

"Serious question though, how did you end up in this life?" I asked.

"How much time you got?" I could tell he was trying to stall this conversation.

"Boy, if you don't stop. I got all the time for you." I gave him a look that would've taken him right out of his clothes if I could.

"You better stop, you gon start something you can't finish," he replied.

"Nah, let me stop then because I know that our sexual chemistry match, but I just wanna get to know you now." I was completely honest with him. Just because you have good sex with someone didn't mean you'd have a good relationship. It was best to learn about each other now before too much time was wasted.

"Well, my father was a drug dealer and my mama was basically the standard first lady. She made sure his money was right; she stayed in the newest and finest threads. But, eventually, my father got caught up and she pretty much got lost after that. She spent days in bed without showering and, at that point, I had to decide. The only good thing was since I'm an only child, I didn't have to focus on anyone else but my mom. Against my father's better judgment, when I was 13 years old, I searched his entire office and found his plug's information. Then, it was pretty much from then on smooth sailing. I have a great relationship with my plug. I still went to school, graduated and everything. I was a true definition of a hustler."

"You still are, from what I can see. How'd you meet Pax and them?" I asked.

"We graduated together. When I raised 50k alone, I put them on with me because they helped me through some of my darkest times. That's why it hurts that Ice may be working against me, after all I've done for him."

I could tell he was really hurt by this. "I'm sorry Marcus. I guess there'd be no conversation that could be had to fix it huh?" I already knew the answer, but I wanted to see what he said.

"Shit, not at all. I can't just ignore that shit. That mean when he around, I'll have to always watch my back and I can't have that. I already gotta be worried about fuck niggas in Nap. Now, somebody I thought was my brother." He ran his hand over his head, touching those fresh ass waves.

"Well, I wonder how Ti-," I was about to ask about Tia, but he cut me off.

"Don't even speak that crazy ass woman name. I knew she was on some bullshit." He looked flustered.

"What happened?"

"She sick as hell. She wants me." I had to scoot up because I didn't hear him well.

"What you say?"

"She wants me, Bayleigh, like want, want. She came on to me the last time she popped up over the here."

My eyes grew big. "I didn't remember her doing that when she came over here."

"That's because you wasn't here the last time she was. She popped up on me again. The night I took you back to your mom's."

"And you just now telling me?" I questioned.

"What was it to tell? She popped up. I told her ass she was crazy as hell and kicked her ass out."

"Yeah, okay." I rolled my eyes.

"Awww see, you not about to be throwing no tantrums. I'm not sure what you're used to, but I'm a grown ass man. I need you to listen and believe when I tell you nothing happened with that psycho." The bass in his voice wasn't alarming, but it let me know that he was telling the truth.

"I'm sorry. I don't know why it would've mattered; we weren't together at the time," I admitted.

"We were to me and, like I said, I'm a grown ass man. I don't have time to play games. I want you and only you. Nobody will be ever take your place." I started blushing, so he placed his hands on my hips and guided me onto his lap. We started kissing and I felt the moisture growing in between my legs. He had something over me; with one touch, he could bring me close to an orgasm. This man was highly skilled and I loved being his task every time. I felt like he learned my body inside and out the first night we had made love. I was definitely in love with this man, but I wouldn't dare scare him off by telling him that so soon. His phone started ringing and I rolled my eyes. I started kissing and licking on his neck.

"W-wwwait, babe, I gotta see who it is. Don't move though." He slapped my left ass cheek and answered the phone.

"Wassup, who is this? Damn, forreal? What hospital he at? Aight, I'm on the way."

He hung up the phone and just stared at me in a weird way.

"Who was that? Who's in the hospital?"

"That was one of Isaiah's runners. They said he in the hospital; he was shot." His face turned another shade and I could tell that wasn't the news he was wanting to hear.

I felt my eyes stinging from holding back tears. "I truly didn't hate Isaiah; I just wasn't in love with him anymore. He was a part of my past. I'd never want anyone to die."

"Even though I feel like that lil nigga was preparing to go to war with me, I still don't know that for sure. So, if he dies and I don't know, then I'mma just keep the memory of him being who he was before shit got so fucked up. I need to go see him." I got off his lap and grabbed my purse, preparing to go with him.

"You sure you wanna go?" he asked me.

"Yes, listen Marcus, we already know we together. I just want to say goodbye to him if this is the last time we'll see him alive. We were friends even before we got together."

"Aight, I hear you. Say no more." He grabbed my hand and we headed out.

***

We stood outside of the ICU room door. Neither one of us really wanted to go in, but we knew we had to see for ourselves.

"What are you doing here?" a guy from behind us said. We turned around and I didn't know who the dude was at all.

"Listen Cee, I'm just coming out of respect. Isaiah know I would never do anything to harm him," Bear explained.

"Did you have to bring this bitch? She's the reason y'all are even against each other in the first place," Cee fired back.

I saw Bear's vein throbbing real hard on the side of his head. I could tell he was ready to pop off on this dude.

"I'mma tell you this one time only, do not disrespect her again. Don't forget. Just because Isaiah is YOUR boss, who was his? Do you really wanna try me right now? We already in the hospital, so they can try and save you quick. But, your best bet is to get the fuck out my face," he said menacingly.

"Sir, if you all don't quiet down, we're going to have to ask you to leave," the nurse came up and said.

"No, ma'am, that won't be necessary. I'm just seeing my brother," Bear responded to her. That was the perfect chance for us to go in and see him and then get the fuck outta here.

When we got into the room, I don't think either one of us expected for his injuries to be more than a single gunshot wound. We heard him squirming, so we went over to his bedside.

"Bay-Bayleigh?" he asked when he saw me. "What you doing here?"

"Well, we got the call that you were shot and we wanted to come and see if you were okay." I tried my best to have some joy in my voice.

"We?"

"Yeah bro, besides the petty bullshit, I just wanted to see if you were doing alright."

Isaiah paused a long time before responding, "He paralyzed me, man. I guess this is my karma for going against someone that looked out for me."

"Who the fuck did it?" Bear questioned.

"Man, I don't even wanna say. I knew the shit was a bad idea from the jump." He just put his head down and shook it.

"Bro, you tell me what's going on and I promise, I will get retribution for you. I'll even put you trying to go against me behind us," Bear offered.

"It was Ice man. He going fucking nuts sniffing y'all product. It makes him a whole different type of dude. He's more vengeful. He made sure he shot me to where I was completely coherent, but with the loss of my sense of touch from the waist down." Isaiah started crying. "How am I gon take care of my child now?"

"I'm so sorry, Isaiah." Tears started falling down my face. His one wrong decision to go against Bear with a madman cost him his life basically. He's still alive but couldn't even function on his own.

"Say less. He violated the one major rule that we have. Never turn into the people we were serving. Isaiah, bro, you ain't gotta worry about your baby because I'mma help out as much as I can." Bear extended his hand to Isaiah. Isaiah struggled, but he took it and I guess their beef was done and over with. I mean, in all honesty, Isaiah was no longer a threat.

***

"Hey girl, how's it going back at Bear's?" I asked Syn over the phone. I had stepped out of Isaiah's room to talk to her for a little bit.

"It's fine. I'm sure Pax locked everything up; we went back to his place. It just didn't feel right being in there without y'all."

"I hear you. I'm sure Bear wouldn't have cared though. So, I see Pax is a potential candidate."

"I guess you could say that. I'm not gon say too much; you know he right here," she laughed.

"Oh okay, well, don't let me interrupt you. We just bout to leave from here. I feel so bad Syn."

"Bad for what? For Isaiah? Girl, he damn near brought it on himself."

"Syn, how could you even speak like that? We graduated together. I would never want that to happen to someone I had so much history with."

"I understand that, but he's the past and he did you dirty, so no need to feel bad about it. You can feel sorry for him, but never feel bad about how you felt after he played you."

"I hear you, Syn. I'll talk to you tomorrow."

"Okay, love you girl."

"Love you too."

I hung up the phone with a heavy heart. I heard everything Syn was saying, but she didn't have to be so blunt about it. I hated that I was so soft when it came to shit like this. I wish I could develop the hard shell that Syn embodied. If there was one thing I wished I had from her, it was that. Everything else I was surely confident about.

"You ready to go?" Bear brought me out my thoughts as he walked out the hospital room.

"Yes baby."

"You good?" he questioned.

"Yes." He stared at me like he knew I was lying. "Okay, not really, but I promise I'll get over it. Just need some time."

I walked over to him and stared in his eyes. "Okay, you say you need time. I believe you but, if you having second thoughts about us, let me know now."

"Uh, uh, don't even think like that. If there's anything I was ever sure about, it's us. I just wanna be a strong woman for you, just like you're a strong man for me." I put my hand on the side of his face. He grabbed both of my hands and kissed them.

"Don't change a thing. I love the fact that you wasn't brought up around the type of life I live. It takes me away from it all. One day, you'll be able to see the raw and uncut version of what I do but, for now, I just wanna enjoy being with somebody who ain't just with me for what I can do for them."

This man made me feel so good about myself, and the fact that he had to be hard on the streets but was so sweet to me made me fall in love even more. I smiled at him and we started walking off hand in hand. This shit with Marcus made me think that maybe Isaiah was just infatuation. Because he made me feel things nobody else had.

***

We pulled back up to his house and he started inching out his neck, looking as if something was off.

"What's wrong?" I asked.

"Stay here," he ordered.

He got out the car and pulled out his gun. I tensed up because I didn't know how I felt about my man going into a situation alone. I looked into the glove department and saw there was a gun lying inside. I'd make sure to use it if something weird happened. I heard a gunshot and then my heart fell into my stomach. Fuck this, I was going to see what was going on!

Bear

I saw a figure in my upstairs window when we pulled up. I'm guessing Pax forgot to turn the light off when they left, but I was actually glad that he didn't turn it off because that's how I was able to see the mafucka who had a death sentence today. My front door was slightly open; I pushed it in quietly and headed up the stairs. If this was Ice, then this mafucka got his death wish very soon and without even making a play first. I had this shit all planned out if he was to come against me but, if he wanted to take it there, we could.

Click! Click!

I cursed myself as I felt the cold steel touch the back of my skull.

"Nigga, you might as well gone and pull that trigger because the moment you let me get a chance to blow your head off, I'm doing just that!" I yelled so loud, you could hear my voice bounce off the walls and echo throughout the house.

"Calm down nigga, cause yo ass is definitely slacking, real shit. How the fuck you not gon make sure the bottom half of the house is clear? Just because you saw my shadow in the room upstairs? You ever thought about it being two or more in this mafucka?" I shook my head as Dave made perfect sense.

I turned around and stared him in the face. "You do make sense. I'm tripping hard." Without warning, I pointed the gun at his face. "Or maybe you decided to go along with that nigga."

He started laughing hysterically. "Nigga, now you know I ain't rocking with no damn Ice over you. That nigga coo coo for cocoa puffs."

I joined in his laughter. "Nah, I know. Damn nigga, you probably got Bayleigh spooked. Let me go check on her."

"Nah, I say we test her, see how she coming behind her nigga." Dave let off a shot into the wall from the top of the stairs.

"Aye nigga!" I shouted. I looked at him like I wanted to kill him.

"I'll fix it myself nigga. Nothing a little plaster and drywall won't fix," he chuckled. We waited for what felt like about thirty seconds and Bayleigh came running in with the gun drawn and, even though I could see the gun shaking from where I stood, I knew shawty was behind me 100%. I definitely had a keeper.

"Damn broooo! She came gun drawn!" Dave laughed. We both walked down the stairs, and I took the gun from Bayleigh's hands.

"What's going on? Now, you gotta worry about Dave too?" she questioned.

"Nah ma, it ain't like that. He was just testing me, that's all, and to be honest, I failed but players fuck up," I admitted.

"Oh okay, I was scared to death. I didn't know what else to do."

"You did right sis," Dave said and wrapped his arm around Bayleigh's shoulder. "Is it okay if I call you sis? We just gotta make sure you ain't scared to shoot that bitch."

I walked over to them and moved Dave's arm from around my girl's neck and replaced it with mine.

"Nigga, don't get too comfortable. But, he right bae. If you gon pick that mafucka up, you gotta be ready to use it and I'm only saying that because I don't want you caught up in any situation. I'm tryna keep that shit far away from you though," I expressed.

"I understand but, shit, I thought something was wrong with my man or that he needed backup. I had to come check the shit out. I didn't know it was some type of test."

"It's coo baby. But, Dave, you heard the news about Isaiah yet?"

"Yeah, Pax told me about that shit; Ice is sick as fuck. But, did you expect anything less? The nigga can't work with NOBODY, not even a mafucka who wanted to be against you right along with him. I don't see how you didn't end that mafucka when you walked into his hospital room," Dave spoke harshly.

I felt Bayleigh's body tense up and I made a mental note to check that shit. She was already being weird about it at the hospital; now, she's tensing up when somebody speak against the nigga.

"Yeah, but that nigga ain't a problem no more and don't forget that was somebody I helped along the way. He just made a bad decision."

"Yeah, that cost him a good life."

"I'mma head upstairs and lay down. I don't feel too good," Bayleigh stated.

"Aight, I'll be up there in a minute." I kissed her on the cheek.

Making sure she was upstairs, Dave came over to me. "You sure she over that nigga?"

"Positive."

"Aw okay, just saying, she looked some type of way when I was talking about the nigga."

"She coo. But, we about to call it a night. And nigga, the next time you think you about to just punk me in my shit again, think twice about it." I was dead ass serious.

"I got you." I closed the door behind him and set the alarm in the house. Dave's words kept playing in my mind. I knew Isaiah couldn't give Bayleigh what she needed, especially not now, so why was I tripping thinking she still wanted that nigga? I shook my head and got those thoughts far away from my head. I walked in the room and walked in on her stripping out of her clothes. I got hard just seeing her body from behind. Her curves and angles were so perfect. I walked up behind her and kissed each of her shoulder blades. Her body melted into mine and she gripped my head, as I made my way to her neck planting kisses and running my tongue up and down it. My hands had minds of their own as they found their way in between her legs. She was wet as fuck; I could tell she was yearning for me to give her body what it needed. I stripped out of my clothes.

"Marcussss," she whispered my name softly.

"Yes?" I managed to get out while sucking on her ear lobe.

"I want you in the worst way."

"I want you too." I turned her around and picked her up. She wrapped her legs around my waist and I headed into the master bathroom. She had the shower running and that was the perfect place to please her right now. I stepped in with her hanging on. The water hit her hair and she leaned her head back as the water ran down her body. I kissed up and down her stomach and then took her nipples into my mouth one by one. I heard her loud gasp as my dick penetrated her tight ass pussy. I deep stroked her as her screams bounced off the shower walls. She gripped my head and kissed me. I started nibbling on her lips and she slid her tongue in my mouth. Everything about her was sweet as hell. I was addicted to her, no doubt, and there was no turning back; I was hooked. I pinned her against the wall and slid out of her. I got down and grabbed one of her legs, putting it on my shoulder. I feasted on her pussy as if it was the last meal on Earth, but I made sure to do it delicately. See, I didn't play when it came to pleasing a woman I was in love with. I wanted them to feel me even when I wasn't in their presence. That's how you knew you were good at what you put down.

"Fuckkkkkk Marcussss, oh, my Godddddddddddd," she moaned. I palmed and squeezed her ass. I felt her warm juices running down my chin, along with the water. I got up and kissed her, letting her taste her own juices. She looked like she was in pure ecstasy. I picked her up and took her to the bed. I got into the missionary position and served her long strokes while sensually kissing all over her neck. I went up to her ear, so she could hear everything I had to say.

"I love you, Bayleigh; you gon be my wife," I whispered. "Fuckkkk, and I'mma make you the mother of my kids. You love me?"

"Yessss," she moaned.

"I wanna give you the world." I knew good sex made a nigga say a lot of things, but I meant every one of them. We both were about to cum and I couldn't wait to hold her in my arms after we was finished. Yeah, she had a nigga sprung forreal.

Ice

Now that I was in this alone with my plan, I had made it my business to take action quickly, probably within the next week. Dave and Pax had made it clear that they wasn't fucking with me anymore. It was just crazy because everything happened so fast. To be honest, Isaiah was the one who came to me wanting to go against Bear. At first, I wasn't gon take him up on the offer, but then I started thinking of how it'd be if I was the only one at the top. I had to admit it seemed like it'd be lovely. But, now I'm questioning if the shit was even worth losing my family over. On the outside looking in, people would say I was cold-hearted and selfish. They were right. It was too late to turn back and apologies wouldn't be able to fix everything at this point. So, I was preparing to go out guns blazing because I knew Bear wouldn't make it easy for me.

Right now, I was in the warehouse in Park 100 cleaning my gun. I would come here late at night because no one else was here. Sooner or later, Bear would be requesting that I give up all the keys I had to his warehouses and storage units. Little did he know, those storage units would be empty come morning. I woulda did it tonight, but the gates were locked and I was too busy fucking this bitch earlier to realize what time it was. So, I figured going in the morning would be best and I'd be able to blend in and not look suspicious. My phone started ringing; I looked and it was my soon-to-be ex-wife.

"What you want Tia?"

"Really Ice? So, how is your family supposed to survive?"

"I don't know what you mean."

"My bank account is frozen! You know what you did! Save the bullshit and just tell me why you would do something to that caliber!"

I rolled my eyes and stared at the phone like it was poison.

"HELLO?!?"

"Look, the moment we said we were divorcing was the moment y'all stopped being my responsibility."

"Are you fucking kidding me?! These are OUR children; I didn't have them alone!"

"Shit, you might as well had. You was clearly trying to trap a nigga and, at one point, I loved yo ass, so that's why I never had shit to say."

"You are going to rot in hell Ice and I promise you that. I can't wait to let Bear know every move you plan to make. Oh, and it'll be nice having another man provide for your children. I mean, how do you even sleep at night? The shit is ridiculous."

"Yeah, aight bitch."

I hung the phone up dead in her face. She was just trying to get under my skin and, plus, she knew nothing of what I had planned. The shit had changed since we separated. I looked at the warehouse one last time; I'd never look back again. I turned off the lights and left the key in the door after I locked it and pulled the fuck off.

***

Today was gon be a great day and I was happy as hell on my way to the storage unit. Bear kept all the extra work stashed there and even had a couple safes filled with money inside as well. Arriving to the storage unit, I put the gate code in and prepared to pull up to the unit. Good thing it was all the way in the back corner so, that way, we'd never really be seen. Bear had paid the storage manager money to keep the cameras off that particular unit. I backed my truck in so that I'd be able to place everything inside the trunk.

I was so anxious to get this shit done in a quick manner. I dropped the keys to the ground and, when I got down to pick them up, that's when I felt something cold pressing into the back of my head. I was too focused on the task at hand that I didn't even pay close attention to my surroundings. I should've known that Bear wouldn't lose too easily.

"Nah, go ahead and finish what you was doing. Open the unit," I heard Pax's voice.

"Aye man, what you on? I'm just putting some money into the safe." I tried my best to provide a reasonable explanation.

"Nigga, open the fucking unit!" he ordered. I didn't even rebut. I took the lock off and pulled up the sliding door.

"Well, well, well, it's about time you arrived; we was starting to suffocate in this mafucka. If you would've waited any longer, you might've gotten away with this greasy ass shit you was about to pull," Bear spoke in a callous manner. My eyes grew wide as him and Dave stood there. The storage unit was completely emptied out; all that you saw was a chair in the middle of the unit and stuff to tie somebody up.

"What y'all got going on? I was just bringing money into the safe."

"Drop the act mafucka. You could at least be a man and stand on that shit. Did you think after you tried to kill Isaiah that he wouldn't provide us with all the information we needed? I'm just trying hard to figure out why you would go against somebody who damn near set you up for life, my nigga?"

See, that was that shit right there. I couldn't stand how he just made it seem like I owed him my damn life or something. He may have given me the shit to start up, but the fact that he's acting like I was indebted to him has my blood boiling.

"Nigga, FUCK YOU!" I shouted. "I'm so fucking sick of you throwing that shit up in our faces. That's why I went against you; I want my own shit set up. I'm tired of working up under yo ass." My words were laced with venom. My true colors were showing and I didn't give a fuck anymore. I hated this nigga for years now.

"You got the shit confused, my nigga; don't mistake me speaking facts as throwing some shit in yo face. Y'all already have yo own shit going on with your teams and all that. All we do is come to the same fucking place to store the money. I'm not cutting y'all checks, the fuck. Y'all get your money from your own teams and disperse them and keep the rest! Do I ever ask for a fucking dime! NO! Nigga, I fucking took care of your kids and wife when you did your bid! We stood by your ass 100% and you feel like you don't have any fucking power?! Seriously?" Bear started chuckling. "Matter a fact, all this talking is really un-fucking-necessary."

"Nigga, you damn right it's unnecessary because I said what the fuck I said. You can keep acting like you not throwing shit in our faces and that you don't feel entitled, but you do and they will see the shit soon enough. Oh, and don't think I didn't know you was sticking your dick in my wife while I was away bitch." This nigga didn't think I knew about that shit, but I fucking knew. Tia and him were way too cozy and she'd say his name more than often. Shit, one time she even called me his name while we were fucking. That's the underlying reason why that bitch got cut off. I cut those kids off, and now I was cutting these mafuckas off because they had me fucked up. If she was messing with Bear, how did I even know they wasn't fucking around back after we graduated high school when she started having kids?

All them niggas just stared at me with a confused look on their face; even Pax came to the side of me and looked at me fucked up. Then, out of nowhere, they all just burst out laughing.

"Are you forreal? Don't nobody want that psychotic ass bitch. I can't help if I'm just who I am. I've always been a woman magnet, but I've made myself clear to your wife several times. That you were her husband and you were like a brother to me. So, that ain't on me," Bear replied in nonchalant tone. Yeah, I knew this was the end of the road for me because I wasn't bowing down to this shit.

"Listen, get it over with. You mafuckas not about to change my mind. I know y'all had some shit going on. It'll come out sooner than later," I said.

I felt a hard blow come across my head.

"Nigga, get yo ass inside," Pax said and pushed me to the ground.

"Y'all sure about this?" Dave asked.

"Oh, you having second thoughts now too?" Pax questioned him.

"Nah, I'm coo. I'm just saying, ain't no turning back from this shit," he responded.

"He became an enemy once he proved he wasn't loyal to us. So, we know what we have to do now," Bear added. He walked out the unit and didn't even look back.

"Fucked up it had to come to this my nigga, but you gotta be the example. You, for one, know that anybody that try and come against what we got going has to be put down."

I looked at Pax real hard and hawked up as much spit into his face that I could muster up. "Fuck you." That was the last thing I said before they started beating the fuck outta me. All I could feel was my ribs cracking, my teeth being knocked out, and eyes getting swollen. These mafuckas was gon leave me here to have a slow and painful death. The last thing I saw was Pax saying one last thing to me.

"Oh and, nigga, it wasn't Bear you had to worry about. I fucked your wife, and I may even be one of them lil nigga's daddy." After that, everything went pitch black.

Bayleigh

"Bayleigh, calm down. I'm sure Bear had a good reason that he was gone when you woke up. Shit, Pax was too, so I'm sure they're together."

I rolled my eyes, as Syn was talking to me on the phone.

"That's not even the point Syn. I just feel like something weird is going on. And with what happened to Isaiah, who's to say nothing won't happen to me cause I'm with him?"

"B, stop. Why all of a sudden you're second guessing y'all relationship? You knew who he was from jump girl. From what I hear on the streets, he's a protector more so than someone who looks for trouble."

"I know, Syn. It's just that since we've been with each other, I'm spending less time with mama; I haven't even thought about what I wanna do with my life. I'm just losing myself I guess."

"Well, have you talked to him? As big of a house he got, maybe y'all can just move in with him. And as far as what you wanna do with your life, you have him by your side. I'm sure he has no problem providing you with a business of your own."

"When did you get so logical and shit?" I was cracking up because Syn was schooling me, when it's usually the other way around.

"Girl, just because I'm street smart don't mean I don't know shit."

"I ain't even mean it like that, but what you doing?"

"Nothing at all. Just got Jr. ready for school, about to drop him off and then come back and get some rest."

"Have you talked to your mama?"

"Girl, no, and I don't plan on talking to her, so please don't ask again."

"Syn, that's your mother."

"And in her case, she only got one daughter. And she chose him over me. She knows all the pain I went through and still decided to choose him. Doesn't matter if it was years later. You can't just look past a father molesting his own daughter."

"You right. I don't know what made her do something like that. She's a beautiful woman. Why would she settle for him and not give one of those guys from the church a chance?"

"Bayleigh, because she's not willing to open herself up to someone new. She'd rather be alone or settle for my father, and that's sad."

"Yeah, it is. Well, good thing you got Pax. I can tell that he doesn't play about you. I'd hate for your daddy to wanna have a reunion and Pax is around."

"Yeah, that'd be ugly as hell. I already told Pax to not hesitate if I was ever in that situation. I just don't want him to go off and do something to him behind my back."

I got quiet and my mind started drifting.

"Bayleigh, hellooooo, Bayleigh? You still there?"

"Oh shit, my bad girl. I just got to thinking about why we got dealt such a shitty hand with life. My mama is dying, you've been molested; it's just fucked up."

"Yeah, it is, but that's why we can't dwell on it. We can only get better from here on out. Look at us, we both found someone to love. It's okay to question it because the shit did happen quickly. But, who said it had to be a time stamp on love? People be knowing each other for years and have yet to experience real love. They think they in love but, really, they not in shit but a bad situation and now their time was wasted. I feel like we won't waste any time. If it turns out that Pax and Bear are not the men for us, then, hey, we still have time to find someone else. We're young."

By this time, tears were flowing freely down my face. I never saw Syn in this type of light. She was always so into hustling and playing men for her next dollar. I felt so bad for even second-guessing her and not seeing how intelligent she really was.

"I love you, girl. You just made my day."

"I love you, too. Now, can you please just enjoy life? Bear is an understanding man. If you let him know that you're feeling disconnected from your life before him, I'm sure he will understand and try and help."

I heard the door to Bear's house open. "Okay, Bear made it back. I'll talk to you later."

I hung up the phone and felt my palms getting sweaty. I didn't know how Bear was gon react to me wanting help with my mama. I mean, I heard what Syn was saying, but I didn't think me and Bear were ready to live together just yet. I was just gon let him know that I needed to go back home for a little bit.

I watched as he walked in and plopped on the couch. He ran his hands over his face and just shook his head.

"What's wrong babe?" I went over and sat next to him, rubbing his head.

"Shit, I just had to kill one of my best friends, well my used-to-be best friend. Like, don't get me wrong. I don't regret that shit, but it still hurt, you know?" I saw the somber look upon his face.

"I'm sorry baby." I laid my head on his shoulder.

"It's okay. What's wrong with you? The conversation you was having sound serious."

"I mean, it kinda is, but I don't wanna add on to what you're already going through."

"Nonsense. Ever since we met, you've been understanding of me and what my situation is like. I'll always have time to listen to you, regardless of what I got going on, so spill it."

"Well, I just been so busy being up under you that I've kinda neglected my mama. I just wanted to tell you, I'll be dedicating more of my time to her."

"Damn, I ain't even realize it. I'm sorry." He stroked the side of my face.

"It's okay baby. I'm grateful for you; I just want you to know that. If it wasn't for you, my mama wouldn't have gotten the medicine that she needed so quickly." My eyes started stinging because the tears were building up. "Damn, I feel like I've been so emotional. My damn period must be coming up."

"I appreciate you. You keep me grounded and make me wanna get out of this life, especially after today. If this life means losing people I done grew up with, I don't want it no more."

"So, what you gon do?" I asked him.

"I'mma get some more money and then, after that, I'm coo. If Pax or Dave wanna stay in this shit, they can, but I'm more than comfortable and can afford to get out the game at 32."

"I hear that baby. Can you run me back to my mama's?"

"Yeah, I got you."

***

As we turned into my mama's neighborhood, everything hit in slow motion for me. I saw the ambulance, a fire truck, and police cars. Bear couldn't even stop the car good enough before I hopped out and ran on the lawn and went through the caution tape that was surrounding my mother's house.

"Ma'am! Ma'am! You can't come in here! This is a crime scene!" someone yelled. I didn't even give a fuck about what they were saying.

"CRIME SCENE??! ARE YOU TELLING ME MY MOTHER WAS MURDERED?!?!" I screamed. This shit wasn't making any sense. Who the hell would want to murder my mother?? I felt my heart shattering inside of my chest and I completely lost it. Why? Like, was this God punishing me because I been so into my own needs lately? Why couldn't I say goodbye one last time?! That was the last thought I had before I felt myself pass out in someone's arms.

***

My eyes started opening slowly and were burning from the light in the room. I looked around and saw that I was in a hospital bed. The IV was in my arm and I was very confused as to why I was in this bed right now.

"There she is," I heard Bear's voice in low tone.

"What's going on Bear? Please tell me us pulling up to my mama house was a bad dream while I was passed out," I said in a hopeful tone.

He came by my side and grabbed my hand.

"No Bay-" He stopped talking, and I could tell he just didn't wanna give me the answer that was the truth. I just started bawling all over again. I couldn't believe this shit. I really couldn't. The door opened and I hurried up and cleaned my face.

"I'm sorry to interrupt. I'm Dr. Johnson; this is Detective Eric Smith. You were still unconscious when I came in and ran some tests. He just had a couple of quick questions for you, but it's your decision. If you're not up to speaking to him right now, we can ask him to leave," Dr. Johnson relayed.

"It's fine, but what type of tests?" I inquired.

"Just the usual ones. You passed out, so we check your blood, run a pregnancy test, and make sure there's no type of viruses found."

"Oh okay, I see."

"I'll have that information for you though, once he's finished," Dr. Johnson said before making his exit.

"First off, I want to express my condolences about your mother. I just wanted to let you know we're going to do everything in our power to find out what happened."

"Thank you," I uttered.

"I doubt that she had any enemies. Have you all recently came across someone that may have enemies?" I saw how Detective Smith looked at Bear.

"No, why the hell would I bring someone around her who can harm her later down the line? Anybody that was around loved my mother and there's no way the murder could've been pre-meditated," I expressed.

"Well, from the looks of it, she was robbed. So, you're probably right about the murder being pre-meditated, but why now? According to the deed, she has been the owner of this house for almost thirty years now. It's just not adding up, but I tell you what. Here's my card; if you hear anything else, please don't hesitate to reach out." He extended the card to me, and Bear grabbed it. The detective damn near burned a hole in Bear's chest. A few minutes later, the detective left out of my room.

"Do you know him or something?" I questioned.

"Yeah, that nigga crooked as they come. He can act like he cares, but really he just want to prolong the case, so the focus isn't on the crooked crimes he be having going on," Bear explained.

"Well, shouldn't I be requesting a new detective then?"

"It may not be necessary. I'm gonna figure this shit out for you."

"You don't have to Bear. Right now, I need you by my side. I haven't even talked to Syn and, oh, my God, what about her mama..." I started crying again. "She gon be so heartbroken once Syn let's her know. I know she's upset with her right now, but I can't be the one to tell her. I just can't."

"I understand that. I'm here, I just don't know what to do, in a way I feel guilty for stealing the time y'all had left together." Bear put his head down. See, this was what made me love the fuck out of him. He was so selfless and he felt my pain when I was down and out. I scooted over in my bed and patted the spot next to me, so he could climb in with me. He just held me as I cried myself to sleep. I guess I'd just wait until the doctor came back in to open my eyes because when I closed my eyes, that was my chance to see my mama again.

Syn

Hearing my best friend's voice over the phone was very heartbreaking. I could tell that she was fighting back the tears when she told me her mama had passed. I couldn't believe it. Bayleigh expressed how she didn't want to be the one to tell my mama what happened. As much as I didn't want to speak to my mother, I had to because if she would find out from the news before we got to tell her, I wouldn't hear the end of it. She'd damn near find a way to make me talk to her, just to curse me out. I pulled up to her house and sighed very loudly. I wasn't prepared for this, but I needed to get it done while Jr. was in school. My hand felt like it weighed ten pounds as I knocked on the front door. I stood there a good two minutes before she answered.

"Shar? Come on in. How's my grandbaby doing?" she asked, as I made my way inside the house.

"He's good, but no need to try and make conversation; I won't be here long. I have some news to tell you. You might wanna sit down mama."

"Shar, what's wrong? Who died?" She slowly sat down on the couch. Tears started welling up in my eyes. Ms. Gina and my mama graduated high school together; blood couldn't make them closer than they already were. "Shar, tell me what happened."

I took a deep breath and, the moment I blinked, the tears fell. "It's Ms. Gina; she was murdered yesterday." It felt like everything stood still. Suddenly, I heard the most chilling scream I'd ever heard from someone. My mama fell to the floor and bawled her eyes out.

"N-not my best friend Lord, whyyyyyyyy! She was already sick, who would do such a thinggggggggg," she wailed. I broke down too; I got right down there with her and comforted her. Imagine seeing someone faithfully every week for the last thirty years and them being taken away from you.

"Let it out mama," I whispered as I held her head in my arms. We sat there together for about thirty minutes.

Breaking the silence, my mama finally spoke, "Poor Bayleigh. I know she's heartbroken."

"Yeah, I could definitely hear it in her voice," I replied.

"I wonder if they have any leads, like this just doesn't seem right at all."

"Bayleigh said the detective said it looks like it was a robbery because some items were missing, like the jewelry and electronic stuff."

"Okay, but murdering her though? This almost seems as if it's someone that they know. A petty robber isn't going to go as far as murdering an elderly woman." My mama made perfect sense, but we weren't detectives. We could say what we think happened all day along but, truthfully, we'd never know until they figure it out. I helped my mama up off the floor.

"Well, I guess I'll be going now. Jr. gets out in two hours, so I'mma go make a few more runs before that," I stated.

"Why not have a meal with your mama?"

"Ma, you think I'mma just forget that you betrayed me? I just wanted to do the due diligence of letting you know about Ms. Gina before you heard about it elsewhere," I admitted.

"But, can you try and understand my point of view though?" I didn't even want to continue the conversation anymore after she asked that. So, I headed towards the door. I swung it open and there was the Devil himself, my father. There was so much anger that built up inside of me and my skin was so hot from my blood boiling that I could bet any amount of money that whoever touched me would get burned right now.

"Oh, and look who it is?! We done spoke you right up. Excuse me!" I shouted and bumped into him as I walked out the front door.

"Shar, please, can we talk?" my father pleaded.

I spun around on my heels so fast. "TALK?! AND JUST WHAT THE FUCK DO YOU WANT TO TALK TO ME ABOUT?!"

"SHAR! LANGUAGE!" my mother yelled. I just rolled my eyes at her.

"Listen Shar, I understand you're upset, you have every right to be. I was drunk and that's no excuse, but I gotta tell you I'm a changed man. I'd never do anything like that being my true self. You're my baby girl." He tried to reach for my hand, but I yanked it away.

"WAS your baby girl. Everything you just said was contradicting and no goddamn excuse. Burn in hell, the both of you." I looked from my father to my mama. I can tell my words stung her to the core, but fuck it. We just were lying on the floor crying together and not once did she say he was coming by. I was through with her just like I'd been through with him. I hopped in my car and sped the fuck off.

***

On the way to Pax's house, I got a call from Bayleigh asking me to pick her up from the hospital. In the back of my mind, I was wondering why she didn't ask Bear. I guess I assumed he was there with her. I pulled up to the hospital lobby doors and she came strolling out. When she got into the front seat, I didn't move the car because I knew my friend needed a hug. She turned to me and broke down. I hugged her for about five minutes before pulling off.

"Where to?" I asked.

"Don't you gotta get Jr.?" she sniffed.

"He gets out in about an hour. I just want to make sure you'll be okay first."

"Yeah, just drop me off at my mama's."

It was silent on the way there and, then, her phone started buzzing and she kept declining the call.

"Bayleigh, why you not answering Bear's calls?" I questioned. "I know it's none of my business but, yesterday, we were just talking about y'all relationship."

"Syn, I can't even. Ugh."

"What's wrong? What did he do?"

"Absolutely nothing, other than getting me pregnant. And the doctor said I need to make sure I stay hydrated for the baby because that's why I passed out in the first place." She started crying.

"Oh, my God, Bayleigh, congratulations! Why are you crying?!" I damn near crashed when she told me that.

Finally, we pulled up to her mom's house and I parked in the driveway and turned the car off.

"Syn, I can't have a baby right now! I don't have my own just yet. I still gotta get myself together first."

"Bayleigh, nobody is ever really ready to have a kid. You know I wasn't my damn self, but maybe this is a blessing. You lost your mom, but you gained a baby. Imagine how she'd feel."

"She'd be pissed at first, but then she'd love the thought of having her first grandbaby." I managed to get a smile out of her.

"There she go. I bet you haven't smiled all night. Have you told Bear?"

"No, that's why I've been dodging his calls. I don't want him to know just yet."

"Uh, why not?"

"Because, don't you see it? I know it's had to run across your mind at least once." She looked at me in a weird way.

"What you talking about?" I asked.

,"Ever since I met Bear, bad stuff has been happening. Like am I getting punished because of the type of man I'm with?" She put her face in her hands.

"Bayleigh, just because the men we are with are drug dealers doesn't make them horrible men. Just because God wouldn't condone how they make their money, that doesn't mean he doesn't understand it. I mean, don't you think he would've punished them a long time ago if that was such an issue?" I explained.

"I just don't know Syn. Like, I really need to start making money on my own. I'm not about to rely on no man, rich or not. I've already let him make decisions for me and he got me to quit the strip club, but that was good money Syn."

"Oh, trust and believe, I know. Pax tryna be on the same shit. But, I tell you what; we can just get a few nights in to where you can establish a cushion and put it in the bank, then we'll stop. You're not going to be showing a baby bump until some months go by," I said.

"I don't know. I feel like Bear would be very upset about that." She shrugged her shoulders.

"Well, you can't say you wanna make your own money, but then bring Bear up every time you have to make a decision."

She got out the car and stuck her head through the passenger side window. "You right. Look, I'll let you know. I love you and thank you for picking me up. Now, I gotta go and get stuff together and start making calls."

"Love you too; call me if you need me. I'm going to get Jr. and then we can come back here if you want. I'm only one call away."

"I know. But, I just wanna be alone right now and soak everything in. I need to figure out how I'mma tell Bear."

I made sure she was safely inside the house before pulling off. I was sure praying that she looked at this baby as a blessing. It would help her overcome her grief because one thing I could guarantee was that if she's depressed, that baby would feel all of that. Right now, I was gon go get my baby boy and cry my own self to sleep. I couldn't believe the fiasco that my mother was living in. She really thought that all could be forgiven between me and my father, and that shit was dead. I guess I'd have to learn how to live a life without them.

Tia

I watched as the little red car pulled off from Bayleigh's mother's house. I was still shaking from everything that transpired yesterday. I didn't mean to, I swear I didn't. She just scared me. I was only supposed to get a few things to pawn because Ice literally left me and the kids with nothing and, now, he's MIA. I looked in the backseat and saw my William and Mia knocked out and then Messiah in the passenger. We literally been sleeping in the car since that day Ice kicked us out.

I'd been trying to reach out to Bear, but got no response. I couldn't try and come at somebody from Bear's family because they never came around. And I wouldn't dare attempt to steal anything from him because I wanna be with him so bad. I figured that I might as well rob Bayleigh because she's in the spot I wanted to be in. But, I never thought it'd go that far. I was really just afraid. Her mom heard me in her living room and, the moment she said something to me, my reflexes kicked in and I turned around and shot her. I felt like shit. This would be a secret I'd have to keep until I was in the grave.

"Mommy, where are we?" my daughter, Mia, asked.

"Don't worry honey. Mommy about to go and get us a hotel room but, first, I need you all to go to abuela for a little bit okay?" I reached my hand in the backseat and got the piece of hair out of her face.

"But, mommy, abuela's house always smell like feet." She poked her lips out.

"I promise it won't be long. I just have some important business to tend to and, then, we can go and get a room at a hotel that has a pool. This will be our last night in Indianapolis." I smiled at her.

"Last night? But mom, what about all my friends and high school?" Messiah woke up and asked.

Shit, I thought to myself. I hadn't broke the news to my two sons yet that we were moving away. I dreaded having that conversation because I knew they'd be upset.

"MJ, there's nothing here for us anymore," I said to him.

"My name is Messiah and I can't believe you. You know we didn't ask to be here and it was your choice to have a child with someone like dad." His words stung to the core. Messiah had never disrespected me like this before.

"I know your damn name! I'm the one who named you. Now, I do understand why you don't want to be called MJ anymore because your father gave you that nickname but, Messiah, do not disrespect me again. Your father was not always like this! Do you know what all I have to go through right now because of how he left us?!" I yelled, and Mia started crying. "I'm sorry for yelling, but I know y'all look at mommy as being your hero and getting things done, but it's only so much mommy can take."

"I apologize," Messiah muttered.

"All is forgiven. You always can vent to me about anything, but the conversation has to be respectful."

I pulled off and thought about how I was going to come up with a master plan to try and get some more money.

Since I'd been with Ice, I never had to worry about shit financially. He always made sure me and the kids were straight. The way he left us just let me know the coke got to his head. I should've known him smoking his own damn product was gon lead to serious changes in our lives. I guess I'd just have to adapt to being a single mother now.

***

I pulled up to my mother's house and braced myself before going inside. "Now, y'all can get some of your things out the trunk before coming in. Don't bring everything in," I ordered them as I got out the car.

"Well, well, well, it's been quite some time since we saw you, mija." I heard my father's voice and, for a minute, I felt like a little girl again.

"Hey papa." I walked over to him and gave him a tight hug.

"Where's my grandbabies?" he asked. I motioned for him to follow me back to the car. They all were standing by the trunk of my car.

"My God, how long has it been? You all have grown so much." He brought them all in for a group hug.

"It's been three years papa."

"Wow, Tia, if you let this much time go by again, it's going to be a problem," he spoke sternly.

"Yes sir," I replied.

"Alright, now, let's come in and see abuela."

We all followed him into the house and I didn't know what Mia was talking about. All I smelled was fresh tamales and tostadas.

"Manuel, did you take out those boxes?" We heard my mom ask from the kitchen.

"Yes honey. Come here, I wanna show you something," he responded.

We heard her complaining because she had to stop cooking. I see nothing had never changed. She stopped dead in her tracks when she saw us.

"Tia?" She walked up to me and put her hand on my face.

"Yes, it's me." I started tearing up. She hugged and squeezed me while sobbing.

"I thought I was never going to see any of you again." She let me go and started hugging the kids.

"Mommy, I've been calling but, after Ice told me y'all didn't want anything to do with me anymore cause I didn't leave him, I didn't know what else to do."

"That jerk off," my dad said.

"We never said that Tia. And you should have known better than to believe that." My mom looked at me with a disappointed look on her face.

"I'm so sorry. I know we can never get those years back," I added.

"Well, we're not going to worry about that now, are we? I cooked, I made tostadas and tamales; we can have whatever the kids want for dessert too." She smiled.

"Mom, can I talk to you in private for a minute?" I asked her.

"Yeah, sure."

We walked to the back of the house. "Mommy, I need a favor," I admitted.

"What? Is that the only reason you showed up here?"

"No. I knew you were going to say that, but me and Ice are getting a divorce. He didn't leave me anything; now, he's gone. It's like he fell off the face of the Earth. All I need is for you and papa to watch the kids until I go handle the home front. We're planning on moving out of Indiana," I explained.

The look on my mother's face broke my heart. "Wow, so the moment you all come back into our lives, you announce that you plan on leaving us again? Why can't you just stay here?"

"Because if we do, Ice may re-surface. I don't want anything else to do with him. The way he put me and the kids out was disgusting."

"I understand mija, but no running. You were not raised that way. If he thinks he's gonna come here to start some trouble, Papa is prepared for that. We've went over this time and time again. I sensed that you were going through it at home, but I knew we couldn't pop up over there without making it harder for you."

"Okay mama, we'll try it your way. This will actually be good news to the boys. They didn't wanna leave their friends behind. But, there is something I need to go handle and, then, I will be right back."

"You promise?" my mother asked.

"I promise." We hugged, and I went back into the living room and gave the kids a kiss. "Abuela has good news for y'all. I think y'all will be happy after all."

"Mommy, are you leaving?" Mia questioned.

"I'll be right back. I just have to go take care of some loose ends. Don't be too bratty with abuela, okay? She don't play; I hope you remember that," I laughed.

"Yes ma'am," Mia replied.

I loved my mother and all, but living with them wasn't in the plan. We'd stay near them in Indiana, but we could not live together. Closing the front door behind me, I caught a feeling in my stomach that didn't really sit well with me, but I shook it off. I needed to be in the right head space to go over to Bear's and pray that he was feeling generous today.

Bayleigh

I had been dodging Bear. When I woke up that night, he was gone and left me the most beautiful note by my bedside. But, I couldn't bring myself to share the news that the doctor shared with me. I knew he was tripping hard about me not responding back to him. But, I planned on going over to his house after I got done dancing at the club. I was gon admit everything and let him know that I'd be starting back working at the strip club, but only for a couple of nights out the week. When Syn and I arrived at the club, all the niggas' eyes were on us for sure. They clearly missed us and we couldn't wait to take their money. I couldn't lie; I was ready to just let go and get my mind off everything that had been going on. All day today I had been planning my mama's funeral and I still got no updates from Detective Smith. We headed to the locker room and saw that are booths were untouched.

"That's crazy that we still had our spots reserved," I laughed.

"Girl, cause look at them other hoes and look at us. They was praying for us to come back. Smitty was blowing my phone up," Syn chuckled.

"Girl, you done gave the owner some punanny or something if he been on your line that hard." I sat in the chair and started putting my makeup on.

"Hell nah, that old ass nigga. I'm good."

We both started laughing together, and this one girl walked in and sighed extra loud.

"Who's that?" I asked Syn.

"That's Tiffani," Syn said. "AND SHE CAN REALLY GET SLAPPED IF THERE'S A PROBLEM," she added in loudly.

"Look, I don't know who you bitches think y'all are, but we were doing just fine without y'all," Tiffani stated.

"Oh, you were bitch? Girl, get the hell on. Them niggas don't wanna see you. They just tolerated your ass because we were on vacation."

"Vacation? Bitch, please, we all know y'all came up off some rich niggas. Miss Doll face here just better be lucky she got Bear before me," she said in a seductive tone.

"What you say?" I turned around so fast, but Syn grabbed my arm.

"The baby," Syn whispered.

"Keep my man's name out your mouth hoe," I said before going back to minding my business like I was before the trick came in. She just walked away, and we finished getting ready.

***

"Calm down everybody. Look, we got something special for y'all tonight. She took a little break after her debut. I know that's weird, right, but she's 100% worth it. She gives everybody a show and, now, she back to make y'all remember her name. Give it up for, Honey!!!" DJ Beats said through the mic. I was lowkey pissed though at that weird comment he made, but I'd let it go for now.

"Oh, na, na, what's my name? Oh, na, na, what's my name?" Rihanna's *What's My Name* came blasting through the speakers. This was a more upbeat dance I was preparing to do, but I wanted to make a statement, especially since that bitch had so much mouth. I started gyrating my body to the beat and running my hands through my hair. I grabbed the pole and swung around it while wrapping my legs around it. I turned upside down and glided down the pole. When I got back up, my heart fell into my chest. I saw Bear in the VIP section and he looked angry as hell. I immediately ran off the stage, so I could get my stuff and leave.

"Girl, what happened?" Syn ran behind me from the hallway.

Tears immediately came down. "Bear is out there; what I'mma do? I haven't spoken to him yet!"

"Oh shit, was Pax with him?" Syn's eyes got wide as hell.

"Girl yes! And Dave. So, you know Bear is damn near gon be done with me now that his friends saw me in this light again. Especially after he spoke about how he didn't want me back here." I was so frantic. I grabbed my phone and he wasn't calling, so what the fuck? He was gon be even more pissed because I was dodging his calls but had the nerve to sit there and come strip again. Yeah, I just knew our relationship was gone be done for and, now, I was feeling stupid as hell.

"Fuckk, nope, uh, uh, we going out the back way." Syn grabbed the keys, and we both grabbed our bags and prepared to go out the back door. I looked the other way to make sure nobody was coming.

"We clear."

Syn opened the back door and ran right into somebody's chest. She was about to fall, but I caught her.

"Busted. Did y'all really think we was gon let this shit slide? And the back door, really? Syn, you coulda came up with a better plan with that. Ain't you the street smart one?" Pax fired questions at us.

"Where's Bear?" I wondered.

"Oh, you in deep shit, and you ain't been answering my nigga's calls either. He very upset. If I were you, I'd be making my way to him and quick," he laughed.

Syn hit him in the chest. "It's not funny Pax, dang. Come on, girl, I'll take you over there."

"Nah, you ain't, you coming with me. And even though yo punishment might be pleasureful, I'm still pissed at you." He licked his lips at Syn.

"First of all, ewwww. Second, of all, how I'mma get there then? You know I don't have a car," I said.

"Here, damn, take mines. He done got me all hot and bothered now." Syn cheesed and handed me her car keys. I just shook my head and pulled off. I prayed that he could forgive me, but I'd understand if he didn't. This was just too much bullshit to be going through. I done almost forgot that I was pregnant with his child. Imagine how his response would be once he found that out and I was literally just on the stage dancing. I'd say a prayer along the way and, hopefully, God looked out.

I started walking to Syn's car and felt somebody following me. I turned around and it was this Tiffani bitch again.

"Bitch, what's your malfunction? Like, I don't even know you."

"I just wanted to say thank you for fucking up your relationship with Bear. See, I for one know how Bear feels about his woman working at this club," Tiffani smirked.

I had a bewildered look on my face.

"Oh, what? You think you the only female he done pulled from this club? Let me guess. He made you quit working the first day, just like he did with my sister?"

"I had enough of this shit." I was about to turn and start walking back to the car.

"Be careful. I'd hate for something to happen. Bear is a good man and he deserves someone who's going to listen to what he tells them to do."

"Are you dumb? For one, you're sick because didn't you just say he was with your sister? And two, I love Bear, but he for one knows that I will never just be that submissive bitch until a ring is on this finger. Not like I have to explain anything to you, but I'm a grown ass woman. Ask him, he knows. So, bitch, you can want my spot all you want. Shit, even attempt to try and take that spot away from me, but it'll never work. He's hooked sis; he can't let me go, even if he tried. And it's okay because I can't let him go either. So, do yourself a favor, mind your fucking business and get yo dusty pussy ass back inside the club." That felt so good. Maybe she got the burnt end of the stick from all my anger, but that's what the hoe got. I ain't even bother to see if she was still there. I just sped off and, hopefully, some of the exhaust got in her damn mouth. Cause that's exactly how she was looking when I pulled off.

I was so amped up now because of that damn girl. Like, why do people go out they way to start shit for no reason? She talking about he her sister's ex, I wouldn't put nothing past her. She probably called him, tryna be on some bullshit and that's how he showed up there. I swear I didn't see him anywhere when we came in. I was sure if he saw me, he would've been on me like white on rice for not answering his calls. I knew I was gon have to make up for this, so I decided to stop by the house and grab some clothes. I even decided to call him myself, but he didn't answer. I understood why though. But, he should at least see where I'm coming from or try and hear me out. Once I had everything I needed, I made my way to his house. I pulled up and saw an unfamiliar vehicle parked in his driveway next to his.

"Now, who the fuck is this?" I asked myself.

Bear

Bayleigh had me so fucked up. I had been blowing down her line for almost a week and she was not replying. Then, the first time I see yo ass, you on the stage at the same club I told you not to work at no more. I thought very highly of Bayleigh and that's why I didn't want her there on that. What's even more upsetting was that that bitch Tiffani was the one who called me there to try and be on some weird shit. I don't know what she thought, seeing that I dated her sister before. I sped home so quick; I swear, it felt like a twenty minute drive got cut down to nine minutes. I was trying to be there for her in her time of need and, instead, she shut me out. I was pissed because I would've been there before the doctor got back in to talk to her, but my plug had wanted to meet earlier than expected and, since this would be my last big run, I couldn't miss it.

I pulled up to the house and there was a car in my driveway. I grabbed the glock off my waist and parked next to it. Nobody was in the car. I got out the mafucking car so quick because who the fuck was in my house at this point? I turned the corner to get to the front door and there sat this crazy bitch on my porch.

"I almost killed yo ass. What are you doing here Tia? Like, am I playing a broken record? You can't just keep coming here."

"Bear, I'm sorry. I really, really need your help," she pleaded.

"Bring yo ass in man." I unlocked the door, and she followed close behind.

"What happened now? What Ice do?" I was preparing myself to get the act on as if I didn't know that Ice was somewhere dead by now.

"No, it's not that, well, it is. He kicked us out. I don't have anything, literally. Like, no means to take care of our children."

"And you want me to help you? That's not my place Tia."

"I know it's not Bear, but what else am I supposed to do? Like, I know I'm overbearing and I apologize for that, but I wouldn't have came here if I could get help from someone else. I don't need no big amount, just something to help us get started out on our own," she begged.

I was about to pour myself a shot of Hennessey, but said fuck it and just drunk it out the bottle.

"Look, I got a lot on my mind. I really don't need this shit," I said in an irritated tone.

"What's wrong?" she asked.

"It don't even matter, just have a drink with me to this crazy ass life we living in." I poured some in a glass and extended it out to her. She grabbed it and threw the shot back. I killed the rest that was in the bottle and I stared real long and hard at her before going to my bedroom. I opened the safe in the closet and pulled out two stacks of $10,000. I got up and, when I turned around, she was standing there naked.

"Ayeeee, what the fuck you doing? Get dressed man." I covered my eyes.

"It's inevitable, Bear. You've always stayed in your place because I was with Ice, but you know we have sexual chemistry. I know you didn't forget that time you fell asleep at my house when he was locked up." She started walking towards me, and I backed away.

"Tia, that shit is old as hell and I woke up with your dick in my mouth. When I caught you doing that, I got out," I stated.

"Oh, was that before or after your kids were released in my throat?" she smirked.

Fuck. I couldn't even front; she was like superhead. That was a secret I was preparing to take to the grave. But, that was a while ago and I was still with Bayleigh anyway, even though she pissed me off.

"Tia, just gone on man, forreal," I said.

"But, why? Like, nobody will have to find out. And plus, I just wanna feel it one time. Ice wasn't all that great in bed. Come on Bear, it can be a quickie." This bitch literally went into my bed and started playing with herself. Like, it's only so much a man could take.

"Mmmmm, it looks like somebody want me just as bad I want them," she moaned. I knew she was referring to the hard dick I had. That was human nature though. I was about to make the biggest mistake of my life and I hated myself for it. Before I knew it, my clothes were off and I was getting ready to cross that line.

"Yesssss Bear, just like thattttt."

"Shut up, don't talk." I started ramming shawty from the back. Couldn't believe I was really giving in to this bitch, but she was here and I needed to take my mind off my fucked-up life at this moment.

"I can'ttttt help ittt. It feels so good," she moaned.

I grabbed a fistful of her hair and slowed my stroke down, making sure she felt every inch of my rod. That shit was short-lived though. I heard the front door opening. I hopped out of her so fast and scanned the room for my basketball shorts. I walked out of my bedroom around the same time she walked in.

"Bayleigh, what you doing here ma?" I looked at her and her makeup was fucked up due to all the crying I guess she was doing.

"I'm sorry Bear. I didn't think you was gon find out this soon. I was gon tell you," she tried to explain herself.

"Nah, I don't even wanna hear it. You know how I feel about that. You were supposed to be my wife and I can't even trust you," I replied.

"Was? Bear, who car is that outside?" Her voice broke when she said that. Damn, I loved her so damn much, but I felt betrayed; I couldn't even lie.

"What you want me to say Bayleigh?"

"Say that you forgive me and that we can continue to be together Bear!" Her voice shook the damn living room.

"You gotta go Bay. Just go." I started walking her towards the door and I heard another door opening. *Fuck*, I said to myself.

"For real Bear? This what we doing? Not even an hour after you walk out on me, you already fucking somebody else. And, then, it's this bitch on top of that?! Fuck you, Bear!" She walked out and slammed the door.

"Bayleigh!" I yelled but didn't walk out the door. I was hurting, and hurt people hurt people. Doesn't make it right, but she damn near broke my heart. Not too many women get to do that; matter a fact, no woman had done it. She been dodging me like I was not worth her time and that was fucked up. I know I made a mistake and I see it more now than ever that what she did I'd be able to get past, but I was not so sure she'd get past this.

I had a lot of firsts with Bayleigh and, even though this was our first major fight, it was also the first time she betrayed me. I turned around and nearly burnt a whole in this bitch Tia's chest with my eyes. "Did I tell you to come out the room?"

"N-no, but I heard another female's voice out he-," This bitch had the audacity.

"Tia, your best bet is to get the fuck out. NOW!" my voice roared and she damn near jumped out of her skin as she dispersed in the room to get her shit, I assumed. But, after some time, she never came back out. I walked into the room and she was in there sitting on the bed crying.

"Bruh, please tell me what you crying for? My girl just caught me making the dumbest mistake of my life with your crazy ass." I took my anger out on her.

"It's something I have to tell you. It's been weighing me down and seeing her just made it worse," she sniffled.

"What?"

"I killed her mother. It was me."

Fuck, not only did I just make a mistake by sleeping with this bitch. When Bayleigh finds out what she did, it's gonna be impossible to rekindle any damn thing with me and her.

"WHAT?! What the fuck would make you do some shit like that! What did that woman or even Bayleigh ever do to you?!?!" I was seeing red; spit was flying out my damn mouth.

She just started sobbing uncontrollably. "I'm so sorry. I swear, it was an accident. I just had been watching y'all to make my best move and that's how I found out where Bayleigh stayed. I needed money. I couldn't rob you; I didn't know what else to do. It was a dumb mistake, I know."

"Bitch, a mistake? You took a woman away from her child. You, as a mother, should know that's fucked up. Like, you and Bayleigh barely even know each other." I tried to make some sense out of this entire situation.

"But, she has what I want. So, yes, I went after her home. I wanted to try and break her momentum up since she's so perfect in your eyes," she scoffed.

"Want what?!"

"YOU!"

"For the last fucking time! We don't belong together. You were my nigga's bitch, that's it, that's all. Everybody done ran through you!" I yelled. I wasn't typically the disrespecting women type because that's not how I was raised, but this bitch was ruthless, and I felt like shit for sticking my dick in somebody so worthless. It had to be the liquor or something cause why would I even fall for the shit?

"I understand you're upset, but you don't have to get so fucking rude. It was an accident!!!!!!!!!!! I didn't mean to kill her mother; that wasn't my intentions!!" she screamed.

"What??" I heard Bayleigh ask. I didn't know when she got back in the house, maybe in the midst of all the yelling me and Tia were doing.

"Bayleigh, go in the living room. Come on." I tried to grab and block her from getting to Tia.

"So, you defending this bitch and she the reason my mama gone?! BITCH, I WILL KILL YOU." She damn near jumped over my shoulder to get to this bitch. All you could see was Bayleigh's fists plummeting in Tia's face over and over again. I figured it was a good way for her to release her anger, and it was well deserved. Finally, I pulled her off of her and Tia laid there, bleeding on the ground.

"Get off of me, Marcus. Don't even fucking touch me." She threw her hands up like I was poison and grabbed her bag off the ground. I followed her to the door.

"Bayleigh, please don't leave. I made a mistake. We can get rid of this bitch right now! I didn't know any of that before ten minutes ago!" I was gon try my hardest to prevent her from leaving me, man.

Her voice started shaking as she spoke, and I was so pissed with myself. "You know, I cam-me here to apologize for going back to the club without you knowing because I get it. No nigga should want they woman flaunting they goods around for others to see. But, the fact that you didn't even wait an hour to go and try and replace me, that's the part that's fucking with me. And on top of that, she's the one who killed my mother. Accident or not, she did it. Now, what am I supposed to do? All this stress will probably kill the baby. I'm just tired."

Wait, did she just say a baby.

"Wait, what you mean this stress will kill the baby? What baby?" I questioned.

"Fuck."

"What baby Bayleigh?" My voice got more demanding for a damn answer.

"I'm pregnant Marcus."

"When did you find out?"

"That night, at the hospital."

"And this is why you haven't been answering my calls?"

"Yes."

"Wow. So, were you thinking about getting rid of it, or you just was gon forget about me and not tell me at all?" So, many thoughts was running through my head right now because why didn't she tell me?

"I'd never kill my baby. And I just didn't know what to say. I feel like I lost myself being with you. Not saying it was your fault, but I lost a lot of time that could've been spent with my mama and, if I was there, maybe it wouldn't have happened. I have to carry that burden every single day."

"No, you don't. Look, we can get rid of Tia and start our lives somewhere else if you want." I grabbed her hands. "I don't want this child to be raised in a single-parent household, you know that."

"You have no choice. Seeing her come out that room like that broke my heart. How am I supposed to get past that?" She looked me in my eyes and, for once, I didn't even have a response. Not a good one anyway. I fucked up. This was definitely on me. Regardless of how I felt, we never even got a chance to speak about any of it and the moment she saw me, it's in this predicament. She let go of my hands and the tears flowed freely down her face.

"I love you, Bayleigh, and that will never change. I promise to God I'm gon fight for this and I want to be there for you, for our child, every step of the way."

She took a deep breath and exhaled. "I will keep you updated. Goodbye Marcus."

I fell to the ground when that door closed behind her. I was about to cry because this was the love of my life, my soul mate; I knew it from the moment I laid eyes on her. Why couldn't my pride let me cry while she was here? Maybe she would've seen that I'd be lost without her. If I could turn back the hands of time, I would've never let this bitch in. Welp, now, she would feel the wrath of causing a lifetime of pain to the love of my life and for fucking up our relationship. I know I played a part in this too, but Tia knew what she was doing. Since her life got turned upside down, she decided to spread that amongst everyone else and I was sick of the shit.

***

I looked down into the eight foot hole I just dug up with Tia's limp body inside of it. She was still alive, barely. I didn't even have to do anything. Bayleigh completely blacked out on her. Every time Tia had tried to regain consciousness, she slipped back out of it. I started filling the hole up with dirt and her face was still partially visible.

"B-Bear, pleeease." I heard her whispering, begging for her life.

"No, not this time Tia. You don't get to try and beg your way out of this. You're a burden and I'm sick of it. At this point, those kids will do better without y'all. Ice is gone too. May y'all both rot in hell," I said all while tossing the dirt in. After a while, I couldn't hear the pleading any longer and a weight lifted off of my shoulders. This was the best and only thing that could be done.

Pax

I couldn't believe I had fell in love with a woman like Syn. I mean, I been in love with shorty the very first day. I couldn't even lie; she put that pussy on me and got me sprung right away. So, when she told me about what her father did to her, my blood was boiling. I wanted to go find that nigga right then and there, but she asked me to not get involved.

There was no way I wasn't getting involved. This nigga really needed to be dead but, at the end of the day, that was still her father. I'd been trying to find this nigga and finally got a hit from one of my stings I serve that work for the social security office. I waited until Syn and Jr. was asleep before I went out. He stayed in this little house off Medford in Haughville. I was parked in my all-black Chevy Caprice and watched him pull up in his driveway in a beat up Dodge Durango. Once he made it out the car, I creeped up the driveway. He went inside the house and closed the door right behind him. I went up to the door and it definitely was locked.

"Fuck," I said to myself. I looked around the porch and there was a flower pot filled with dirt. It must've been my lucky day because there was a key there. Well, that was the oldest trick in the book, so I made my way inside and his eyes popped out of his head.

"Who-who are you?" he asked.

"Your worst nightmare. You've hurt someone very dear and important to me. Now, under different circumstances, I'd be here to make you disappear but, since you are who you are, I can only offer you a deal." I cut right to the chase.

"What deal? What are you even talking about? Young man, get out of my house before I call the police." He jumped up off the couch.

"See, now you bring the police into it and I'm sure Syn would be understanding as to why I killed her father at that point." When I mentioned Syn's name, his facial expression changed.

"My daughter, sent you here to kill me?" He was shocked.

"Nah nigga, she didn't send me at all but, shit, if she did, it would be well deserved. What type of man are you to lay hands on your daughter inappropriately? That's sick as fuck."

"I don't need you to judge me. I've made my bed and have to lay in it. I used to be an alcoholic and I already apologized to her multiple times." He sat back down on the couch, grabbed his remote, and started flicking through channels on the TV.

"Nigga, you think it's a game." I dug into my waistband and pulled out the Glock that was lying there waiting. He instantly dropped the remote and put his hands up. He even started crying like a little bitch.

"Pl-please man, I'm tryna get my life right," he begged.

"You real lucky because I really wanna empty the clip in your perverted ass but, instead, I'm gonna offer you

$50,000 to leave this fucking state. Get the fuck away from Syn and her mama."

"I can't, I can't," he said all while shaking his hands uncontrollably. I cocked my gun back and he started pleading even more. "Alright, alright! I'll leave. I just hope one day they'll understand."

"Ain't no understanding nigga, they better off without you. The moment you call this phone and let me know your arrangements, that's when you'll get the money. I trust that you'll make the wise decision and choose not to test me." I put the gun back in my waistband and made my exit.

When I got home, I got right in the bed with Syn. She snuggled up against me, and I wrapped my arms around her.

"Where did you go?" she questioned.

"Just had to handle something from one of the runners. Sorry for waking you." I kissed the back of her head and we went to sleep.

    ***

It had been almost two days since I heard from that nigga Bear and that shit was not normal. I decided to pop up at his crib. His truck was in the driveway, so what the hell was going on? I started banging on the door like the damn police. He opened it up, and I swear this nigga was looking bummy as hell.

"Nigga, what the fuck is wrong with you?!" I was confused as hell walking through that damn door. It was junky in the house and all that; this nigga ain't never lived like this.

"Man, what you want?" He slammed the door and plopped back on the couch.

"Don't make me call your mama over here bro. Like, this shit is unacceptable."

"Man, I just ain't been feeling it lately."

"You got the heartbroken bug." I started laughing hard as hell. He just stared at me like I was the lamest nigga on Earth right now. "Nigga, you don't need to look at me like that. You the one over here sick as hell without Bayleigh."

"Man, she really done with me, bro. I've called and called, texts and voicemails. Nothing. Shit, I even been sending her gifts and shit for the past two weeks."

This shit was a sight to see because I never saw him sweating over a female this hard.

"Well, you damn sure ain't gon get her back looking like that. You know my housewarming is tomorrow. Why don't you just come through and make your move then?" I suggested.

His eyebrow raised and he looked like the light bulb went off inside his head. Suddenly, he jumped up. I damn near squared up cause he caught me off guard.

"Hell yeah, I'mma propose," he said calmly.

"Propose? Damn nigga, I ain't say all that."

"Nah, fuck that. I know what the fuck I want and that's Bayleigh Marie. I don't even need to think twice. Plus, she will know that I ain't playing the fuck around. I'm ready to get our damn lives started. I'm glad you came over though because I been meaning to talk to you about something." He sat back down.

"Wassup?"

"I think it's about time that you take over completely. I'm done man."

"Nah bro, you know you ain't done." I never thought the day would come that he'd get out the game.

"I'm serious bro. You know I was always tryna run it up just to get out this shit. That was my main goal. My mama is doing real well with the restaurant and shit. I got investments, and you and Dave doing good too. I did what I was supposed to do and that was to make sure we all eating."

He was spitting some real shit and I would happily take over because he deserved to live a good and peaceful life from now on.

I held my hand out to secure the discussion and he shook it. "Aight, my nigga, I'mma head out. But, you may wanna get your shit together before coming at sis like that. You know she'll clown yo ass in front of all our guests tomorrow."

"I already know." He laughed, and I left.

Bayleigh

"Okay Bayleigh, we are all done," Dr. Jameson said.

"Thank you." I smiled. When she left out, I got off the bed and wiped the gel off my baby bump. I looked at myself in the mirror that was at the sink and smiled. I couldn't believe these four months had flew by and I was getting ready to find out the sex of my baby next month. I was hoping it's a baby girl. Whatever it is was being very stubborn today. My phone started ringing again and I rolled my eyes. I picked it up out my purse and saw it was Marcus calling again.

"Damn nigga. Like, don't you get it by now," I said out loud. I grabbed my purse and pulled my shirt down over my stomach. When I opened the door, my heart almost dropped out my chest.

"Marcus, you scared the hell out of me." I placed my hand on my chest.

"Nah, fuck that. Why haven't you been answering my calls? You told me the appointment was at 3 p.m. Bayleigh. It's 2:38." He looked at his apple watch.

"Um, can we talk outside dang? You up in here cursing. Let me get my next appointment slip." I made my way past him. Oh, my God, he smelled so damn good. My kitty got to jumping, but I had to shake that shit off. He stood right by me as I waited for the next appointment.

"Who let him back here?" I asked the receptionist.

"Well, he said he was your child's father. Do you want him blocked from coming?" she questioned with an attitude.

"No, it was a joke, but just give me my slip. I don't like your attitude; you must want him or something?" My jealousy was starting to show because the way the receptionist was eyeballing this nigga, that's the real reason she let him back there. She tryna get in good with him. I heard him chuckle a little bit.

"Here you go." She put the slip on the counter, and I snatched it off. He followed me to my new car.

"Oh, so, how'd you get this?" he wondered.

"Well, if you must know, my mama left me a little bit of money when she passed. Money I wasn't even aware of."

"That's wassup. I know you happy. Nah, but cut the games though, Bayleigh. Why would you do that? I told you I wanted to be a part of everything with my child." His vein was popping out the side of his head. These hormones was a mafucka because I was ready to get it in with him. I couldn't help he just looked so damn good.

"I'm sorry Marcus," I mumbled and tried to get into my car. He blocked the way.

"Look, stop playing ma and come home. Who you tryna prove something to?" He came into my personal space.

"Myself, Marcus. You already knew about the bullshit I went through with Isaiah, and what's crazy is you have everybody looking at you like you're a God and you can do no wrong, but you got caught slipping by a thot and fell for it. Like, that shit is beyond me. Can I get through please?"

"Well, I don't wanna stress you and the baby out, but I never said I was perfect ma. You can't blame me for other people's perceptions of me. I'm a man and I fucked up. I should've known better. I shouldn't have let that broad in my house. But, even though I lost you behind that shit, I'm thankful we found out who did that to your mama. You can't tell me in a way you don't feel some closure. Yes, we will never know why she came after your home which led to that senseless act, but we at least know who did it and she paid for it," he stated.

"Did you kill her?" I honestly didn't care, but I wanted to know if I had to worry about this bitch sneaking up on me.

"Not technically, well, I'm sure she's dead now, but after the beating you left on her, that girl damn near was gone. I just made sure there wouldn't be a trace of her anywhere."

"Okay cool."

It was a brief moment of awkward silence.

"Well, Marcus, it's hot. I'm ready to go home and kick my feet up. I gotta work tonight," I mentioned.

"Oh, so you still work the club?" he questioned.

I gave him a look of death, and he held his hands up in a surrender motion.

"For your information, no, I don't work the club anymore. The fuck I look like dancing in the club, especially after all that's transpired." I rolled my eyes.

"That weight looking real good on you. I bet you look sexy. Shit, you can dance for me." He licked his lips.

"Marcus. Chill. Nah, but I work at the liquor store over on Lynhurst."

"Man, hell nah, you should not be on your feet like that, for one. Just let me do what I'm supposed to do Bay, damn. I'll send you over some money. You really don't have to work another day in your life."

"I'm good Marcus. Now, I gotta go. You saw the appointment slip. I guess I'll see you then."

"What about the housewarming?" he wondered.

"Maybe, maybe not."

He moved out the way, allowing me to get inside the car. I looked through the rearview mirror as I pulled off. All I could do was shake my head. This nigga really thought he could just sweet talk me into getting back with him. I was happy we met up under these circumstances and not at the house because I knew for a fact if he would've had me all alone in a house, with a bed, shit, at this point anywhere in the damn house, I would've folded.

***

When I got home, I took a nap. My phone ringing woke me up.

Groggily, I answered, "Hello?"

"Girl, open the door." It was Syn.

I got out the bed and made my way to the front door to let her in.

"Hey bihhhhh." She came in all joyous.

"Why the hell you so happy?" I asked and went and sat on the couch.

"Cause I just got some dick, I just got some dick ayeeeeee." She started twerking and laughing.

Laughing right along with her, I said, "Girl, gone on with that."

"Don't be hating. You need to dust them coochie cob webs off and let Bear hit that again." She came over and sat by me and started rubbing my belly.

"Please don't bring his name up. We had a field day at the doctor's office earlier."

"What happened?"

"Nothing major. I maybe lied and told him the appointment was at a different time than it really was. He was pissed."

"That was so wrong Bayleigh," Syn commented.

"Yeah, I know, but I couldn't lie. He looked good as hell like a Mr. Goodbar or something," I giggled.

"Yeah, yo ass must want some damn candy talking about a Mr. Goodbar." Syn cracked up.

"He did, man. If we was at the crib, I just know I would've gave him the business right then and there. Pregnant and all."

"Girl, you would really have him hooked then. Pregnant pussy some of the best from what I've been told."

"What you mean been told? When you was pregnant with Jr. or right now?" My eyebrow raised.

"I'm talking about with Jr. You know damn well after I had Jr., I said I was done having kids. I did that shit naturally too; he almost ripped my pussy apart." Syn was dead ass serious.

"How are you and Pax by the way?"

"We good. Real good actually. We had a heart-to-heart the other night because he answered my phone and it was one of my old clients. When I used to escort and shit. He didn't even judge me girl. He just felt like we should lay everything out on the line. Girl, do you know he fucked Tia too. Only they both were very much sober and she just a damn hoe. That was even when they were all still cool with Ice, but Ice was locked up."

"Damn." My jaw dropped I couldn't believe it.

"Yes. She was the true definition of a hoe. When I told him about her doing that shit to your mama, he couldn't believe that shit."

"Yeah. Just senseless as fuck, but karma is a bitch."

"So, are you gon finally take Bear back or what?"

"Why am I always asked that question?"

"Becauseeeeeeee we tired of splitting up to see one of y'all or inviting you over when he leaves and vice versa. Like, we about to have our housewarming for the new house and we want y'all there at the same time."

"I mean, I'm not saying I can't be around him Syn, I'm just saying the likelihood of us getting back together is very slim. But, of course, I will be there. I love you, you love Pax, and Pax is Marcus' best friend so."

"Yessss, thanks love. I'm so happy. Oh, and by the way, you know it's tomorrow right?." Syn started cracking up. I just glared at her.

"Really nigga? I gotta get my hair done, my damn feet done. Even though I can barely see them, I want them mafuckas pretty."

"See, now why you worried about your appearance if you so over him?"

"Seeee, I never said I was over him. I'm avoiding him as much as I can because I can't get over him. Girl, I told you he was like my soul mate and I still believe that. I'm just trying to let time play everything out at this point."

"Ohhhh okay, you on some mental or psychological warfare shit."

"Yep, I gotta get inside his mental. Trust me, if Marcus really wants me back, it's only a matter of time before he makes a major move about it."

"Girl aight, don't lose him playing games and shit. This ain't Two Can Play That Game. Remember, she ended up having to crawl back to him."

"Trust and believe, when he sees me in tomorrow, he's gon be the one crawling and that's facts."

"Big facts," she added. It felt so good to get out all these laughs with my best friend. She truly was like a sister to me. I was so happy for her because she was finally settling down with somebody. You could tell Pax made her happy because she had a glow about her that was just so beautiful. I guess it was time that I made a decision on where Marcus and I stood, and I needed to be real with myself. It's crazy because after Isaiah hurt me, I vowed to never let nobody hurt me like that again and be able to get any more of my love or time. But, I couldn't help who I fell in love with and I knew Marcus didn't give two fucks about Tia's ass. And if everybody knew about what she did outside of our circle, they'd definitely be wondering why I was considering giving him another chance. It's not something that could really be explained. One thing we did accomplish from this was finding out what she did. Shit, the detective sure wasn't going to figure it out anytime soon. He called me a month after she died and said they'd have to close the case because they had no leads.

I wasn't even mad though because I already had found out. It just showed that IMPD sucked. They had more cold cases than solved ones, so I didn't really expect anything more. My mama had life insurance and I didn't know nothing about it. She had a $500,000 policy and, little did Marcus know, I was really good on the money tip. I didn't have to work but, sometimes, I would drive myself crazy being up in here all alone. Memories of my mama continued to invade my mind. Sometimes, I'd feel her presence here with me. I guess it was time I decided to either sell this house or rent it out.

I went into the kitchen and grabbed me a bowl of Ben & Jerry strawberry cheesecake ice cream. My phone rang again and I looked at it, confused.

"Hello?"

"Hey Bayleigh."

"Isaiah? What's up?"

"Nothing much, just never really got the chance to call and let you know I'm sorry for your loss. Ms. Gina was a very nice lady."

"Awwww, thank you, Isaiah; I really appreciate that. How's everything with you?"

"Shit, as good as it can be. I did a little physical therapy for the top of my body to get stronger. They said there's some notice of movement in my lower body, but I'm not holding onto that until I get some for sure answers there. Just glad to be alive."

"That's wassup, I hear that."

"Word around town is that you're pregnant."

"That I am."

"Do you know what it is yet?"

"Nah, not yet."

"You and Bear still together?"

I rolled my eyes; I knew that question was coming.

"Isaiah, I take it if you know about the baby, then you know me and him ain't together anymore."

"Yeah, you right. I apologize. I just wanted you to know I'm sorry about everything I did. But, as much as I hate to admit, Bear a good dude; he just got caught up in a fucked up situation."

"Did he put you up to this?"

Laughing, he replied, "Nah. I just know my chances are shot with you and I saw how much you liked him so."

"Well, thank you for those nice words, but we will have to see."

"Okay, I'mma let you go. If you ever need to talk or just need to make a joke or two, I'm here."

"Bye boy."

I hung up the phone in good spirits. It was cool that Isaiah was making light of his situation. For the rest of the night, it was just me, my baby, Waiting to Exhale, and this bowl of ice cream.

***

"Wassup sis?" I was greeted by Pax as I walked inside of his and Syn's new mini mansion.

"This is so dope y'all." I smiled while looking up at the ceiling.

"Thank you, boo." Syn hugged me.

"You want some food sis? I know that baby hungry," Pax laughed.

"What you tryna say? Am I getting fat Syn?" I asked her and looked down at my body.

"Nah, you just right." I heard his voice.

"Nigga, you always so damn smooth. I bet she like fuck it all right now, let's go nigga." Pax was always playing; he got on my nerves. "Come on baby." He grabbed Syn's hands and they walked off.

"You look amazing. Please tell me you wore that for me." Marcus moved the hair out my face.

"Maybe, maybe not. Only time will tell," I smirked and walked away to head to the kitchen. Of course, he was following me.

"What you want baby? I got you. Go take a seat," he ordered.

"You should know, if you know me," I said before going to sit at the kitchen table. I was minding my own business and I saw Dave on the patio by himself in deep thought. I decided to check on him. He and I always had a good friendship since I been with Marcus. I closed the patio door behind me.

"Hey Dave, you good?" I asked.

"Oh, hey sis. Yeah, I'm aight." He barely even looked me in the eye. I knew something was off.

"Well, I don't believe that. Wanna talk about it?"

"Nah, it's not a good time. And it's kinda between us men, you know?"

"Oh, it's something with Bear?"

"Yeah, kinda."

"Awww okay. My bad, I just wanted to check on you. I know you're usually sociable."

"You good sis. I appreciate that though."

I just smiled and walked back inside.

"What was that about?" Bear asked as he came to me with two plates stacked with food.

"Really? Do it look like I'mma eat all that? And I was just seeing what was wrong. He distancing himself from everybody." I grabbed a shrimp skewer off of the plate.

"Awww yeah, something is definitely up with him, but I ain't even gon worry about that today. I'm worried about you." We both sat at the table and he made it his business to sit extra close to me. We were having such a good time, laughing and mingling with everyone. We got complimented on being a good looking couple at least like three times and that did nothing but hype him up.

"I'mma go ahead and go to the bathroom. This baby damn near on my bladder," I whispered to him.

"Oh okay." He stood up, so I could walk by him to get from around the table. I made sure I brushed my ass against him to try and tease him a little bit.

When I made it to the bathroom, I played in my hair a little bit and admired myself in the mirror. I was dressed in an all-black, strapless sundress. It fit me perfectly and made my baby bump not stand out as much as it would've if I was naked. I made sure to wear the diamond pendant necklace he bought for me. I heard a knock at the door, and he came walking in.

"Ummm, excuse me, somebody in here." I smiled hard as hell.

"You knew what you was doing. Brushing up against me like that." He wrapped his arms around my waist and started caressing my stomach.

"When do we find out what sex the baby is?"

"Next month but, to be honest, I'd rather discuss the sex between me and you. And not do so much talking." I turned around to face him and I placed my lips on his. He picked me up and lifted my dress up, exposing my ass cheeks. His strong hands caressed them and held them in the palm of his hand. He sat me on the bathroom sink and unbuckled his Rock Revival jeans. My mouth watered as he pulled out one of the things I missed most about him. He came to the edge of the sink and picked me back up. I wrapped my arms around his head, and he slid inside me. I let out the biggest gasp ever. I hadn't felt him in months. I felt my pussy contracting so much against his dick. My juices were already flowing. I threw my head back and tried my best to keep from screaming. He bit and sucked all over my neck and I was in pure bliss. I didn't know if this shit was feeling better than ever because I was pregnant or because it been so long.

"I missed this pussy so much," he whispered in my ear.

Moaning, I replied, "She missed you too."

"Fuckkkkk," he groaned loudly. I put my hand over his mouth. I met him thrust with thrust and I felt him release all inside of me. We just stayed in that position for a good five minutes.

"Oh, my God, I needed that," I admitted.

"Me too," he replied. He grabbed one of their decorative rags and ran it under warm water. He wiped me down and made sure I was cleaned back up and then himself. He put the rags in the hamper that was located in the corner.

"Syn gon kill us," I snickered.

"No, she ain't. She know it was a long time coming with us."

I was preparing to walk out, but he stopped me.

"Where you going?" He bit his lip.

"Uh, uh, that was just some release we both clearly needed," I said.

"And you expect me to believe that?"

"Yes."

"Well, I got something that'll change your mind." He got down on one knee.

"Marcus! Get up!" I smiled but really was shocked as fuck.

"Nope." He dug into his pocket and pulled out a pretty lavender colored box. "Bayleigh Marie Warren, I truly experienced life at its' worse point when you left me. But, what that showed me was that I couldn't live without you. Every day that I was away from you killed me slowly and just being with you for these couple of hours, I can already see I'm being restored. The best thing I did on that hot summer day was walk into that strip club, where I first saw you. At that moment, I knew you were above the rest and you deserved to be treated like a queen. I promise to show you how perfect you are and always treat you with the upmost respect. I love you so much." He revealed a beautiful four-karat engagement ring with a round cut diamond.

By this time, tears were rapidly falling down my face and I just didn't see how I could say no to this. Syn was wrong, for once. My tough love did work, and he knew that I was the best thing for him as he was for me.

"Yes, yes!" I screamed. He took the ring out and placed it on my left ring finger. He stood up and we shared a passionate kiss. I was so ready to show off my new ring. But, when we opened the door, we didn't even have to go far; Syn and Pax were standing at the bathroom door.

"You know I was wondering how you was gon propose, but I didn't think it was gon be after a quickie in our bathroom." Pax started laughing hysterically.

"Damn so, what, y'all was listening?" I questioned them.

"Damn near. Shit, y'all was about to have us going for a quickie our damn selves," Syn giggled.

"Just sick," I responded. "Look bitch," I said to her and held my hand up.

"Congratulations! I can't wait til we start planning!" Syn hugged me and we jumped up and down.

"Congrats bro. I'm glad y'all finally got it right," Pax said, shaking up with Marcus.

"That's what happens when a nigga put it down. Ain't that right Bay?" He was getting big headed as hell.

"Yeah, okay, they heard yo ass in there too even when my hand was covering your mouth." I looked at him with the side eye.

"I can't even debate with you there."

"Well, come on, let's go celebrate!" Syn grabbed my hand and we walked into the living room.

"Listen up everybody! Say hello to the newly engaged couple, Bear and Bayleigh!!!" Everybody started clapping and I couldn't take this smile off my face. I was truly happy as hell and I hadn't been happy in a long time. This was a summer vibe I couldn't let go of, a vibe that I wanted to keep feeling for the rest of my life. I was truly grateful to be with someone whose name held weight in the streets. Someone who I knew could protect me when it all boiled down to it. I couldn't wait until we brought out child into the world. I know he probably wanted a boy because he always talked about how he wanted to have a boy before a girl, so she could have a big brother. No matter what sex it was, we were gon love and spoil it as much as we could. Life was great and there was no other way around it at this point.

Epilogue:

Bayleigh

"Hey mama, just wanted to give you an update on everything that's happened. I still can't believe you're gone, but you're having a granddaughter. I'm due in about three weeks now. Marcus and I are getting married and I know you was skeptical about him, but we're soul mates. I love him to death. After the rough patch we went through, he showed me how much he needed me in his life, and I need him too. You know I never wanted to raise a child in a single-parent household because even though you never showed me that we struggled, I just don't want that for my child. I came here to say I hope you're not disappointed in me and that I miss you so much. Your new headstone came in and it's beautiful. Fit for a true queen." The tears started rolling down my face as I sat there and realized that my mama was really gone out my life. We couldn't reap the benefits that life had to offer. She couldn't see me become a mother and use the tips that she used for me when I was growing up. I felt Bear's arms wrap around me.

"It's gon be okay baby." He kissed the back of my neck.

"I just miss her so much." I wiped my eyes.

"I know you do. She's proud of you, Bay; the plans you have to keep her memory alive, she's going to love them and I just want you to know I plan on backing you every step of the way. Whatever you need, you know I'm always gon be here for you."

This man had a way of providing me with so much comfort and I couldn't be more happy to become his wife. These last two months had been extremely hectic with making sure the baby was okay, making wedding plans, and even with trying to help Syn take care of her mother. It was the least I could do seeing that my mother was supposed to still be here and I had a lot more to help my own mama with. Apparently, Syn's father left without a trace in the world and her mama went into some type of shock about it. I personally think it was because of my mama dying and, then, her father leaving was the icing on the cake. I knew deep down inside, Syn was happy though. I ain't gon lie; I was too. He shouldn't have came around in the first place.

Bear and Pax had officially made a deal that Pax would now be taking over the organization, and I started to see Dave coming around less and less. It was just something weird going on with him. Bear tried to say it was nothing and that he didn't have an issue with the agreement him and Pax had going on, but come on now. He could easily be jealous. I just wanted Bear to be careful and not make a new enemy. Lord knows we didn't have time for that. But, my baby said we had nothing to worry about when it came to Dave, and I believed that. We decided to plan both my baby shower and bridal shower into one event. I was so stressed, but I was eager to make this event one of the best ones Naptown had ever seen.

"Okay, we can leave now. I just needed to check and make sure her headstone was everything I asked for."

We walked away from my mama's gravesite hand in hand, got into the truck, and pulled right out of Crown Hill Cemetery.

"We have to meet Ebony at the A-Class center. There's just a few more things we need to point out before the big day tomorrow," I mentioned.

"Aight bet. She there now?"

"Yes."

I laid my head back and decided to rest my eyes. I didn't wake up until he opened my door when we arrived.

"Damn, I slept the whole way here," I said to myself.

"Yeah, you were out, snoring and all," he laughed.

Laughing right along with him, I said, "No I was not."

"Yeah aight, yo ass was drooling and all."

"Heyyyyyyyy!!!!!!!!!" I swear, Ebony was always so damn cheerful. She'd been like this ever since we started planning this with her.

"Good afternoon Ebony, how's everything?"

"It's going really well. We have everything decorated for you. The caterers are already preparing the food. Of course, some stuff will be served fresh come tomorrow. Oh, and the cakes have arrived. Follow me," she ordered.

We followed her into one of the event rooms. It was a pretty decent size, but not such a large space. I didn't really mess with my family on either side and I didn't have many friends. Most of these people would be Bear's family. He already prepped me for who all I was about to meet.

We walked into the banquet hall and my mouth dropped; it was so beautiful. We had chosen a white and gold theme because we felt like our lives needed a brightness that our baby girl would bring.

"What you think?" Ebony asked.

"It looks amazing. Thank you so much. We really appreciate it." I gave her a hug.

"I'm glad you like it. Today is about you and your baby girl. May you all have a great time. I will be on standby if you need anything at all." She smiled and walked away.

"You ready to go get ready?" Bear asked me.

"Yes, I just can't believe where we are. I never thought we'd be having a baby and getting married so quickly." I rubbed my stomach.

"I knew it, shit. I wanted you the moment I laid eyes on you. I knew I wanted you to be my wife, have my baby, all that."

Laughing, I said, "Yeah, okay, you just saying that to try and get a quickie or something."

"Nah, I'm forreal, Bayleigh. I was a good man before, but you turned me into a great man. You helped me see that I needed to work on some things about myself and, even though you leaving me was the hardest thing I ever went through, it was worth it because it made me love you ten times more. It showed me how much I couldn't live without you and that I needed you in my life forever."

I was so emotional since I'd been pregnant and the water works was just coming down my fast. I was so happy about our little family and our friends. I was ready to start forever with him.

"I love me some you," I said as we closed in the space between us. He placed his lips on mine and it was by far the most sensual kiss we ever had. I was happy, I was grateful, and I vowed to always keep our family together. This was a vibe I never wanted to give up!

Social Media

Facebook: Nayh Alontrice

Instagram: nayhtheauthoress

CPSIA information can be obtained
at www.ICGtesting.com
Printed in the USA
LVHW111602051120
670844LV00003B/510